# SWITCH BACK

By

Steve K. S. Grey

Copyright © Steve K. S. Grey 2015
This book is sold subject to the condition that it shall not, by way of trade or otherwise, be lent, resold, hired out, or otherwise circulated without the publisher's prior consent in any form of binding or cover other than that in which it is published and without a similar condition including this condition being imposed on the subsequent publisher.
The moral right of Steve K. S. Grey has been asserted.
ISBN-13: 978-1518786532
ISBN-10: 1518786537

*I dedicate this to my wife and children who have shown me the meaning of true love, and without them I would be truly lost.*

# CONTENTS

Chapter 1.  *Life at home – age 0-9 years old* ................................... 1

Chapter 2.  *Life in children's homes - age 9 to 16 years old* ........... 19

Chapter 3.  *My colourful career started on the Rodeo Switchback* .. 56

Chapter 4.  *My life between the Switchback and getting married* .... 73

Chapter 5.  *Marriage, work life, children, and voluntary roles* ...... 101

# ACKNOWLEDGMENTS

I would like to thank my wife Lou for her constant love and support through the writing of my life in the pages of this book, and for being understanding when sometimes the story was very sensitive about past relationships, but understanding these things needed to be said to make the story true to life. Big hugs and xxxx.

# Chapter 1

## *Life at home – age 0-9 years old*

Hi, my name is Steve Grey. When I take you through my life story, sometimes I will write things that I am reflecting back on, or have learnt about later in life, that help fill in gaps in my life.

For example, I did not have any knowledge of where I was born until I was 18 years old, I guess when I was old enough to perhaps wonder where I was born. The question was really irrelevant in my teenage years, when I may have been interested in knowing where I was born.

Anyway, when I was 18 I found out I was born at home at 255 Sunlight Cottage, Hursley, Winchester. It was a little farm cottage tucked away on a big farm; my father was a gamekeeper when I was born. My parents had already had a daughter and son a year and a half older than me and three years older than me, the sister being the eldest.

Now because the life of abuse we grew up with at home, and my life in children's homes, I feel I must write this story using different names to protect the identities of my brothers and sisters and the children in the kids' homes.

So, still using details I learnt when I was 18, to a point I start recalling my younger years, I learnt at the age of 2 years old my family moved to the Green Croft in Salisbury, Wiltshire, to a three-storey end-terrace house, which had an alleyway on the right-hand side, then a Methodist church. Also by then I had a baby brother who would have been 6 months old.

Now to be honest, my recollections of my younger years only go back to 1972.

I say this because I was born on Jan 1$^{st}$ 1967, and the first song that really sticks in my mind is the Long Haired Lover from Liverpool by Donny Osmond, I think, so this means, really, I'm 5 years old during my best memories of my childhood. One of the things I can remember around this time, is that my dad used to drive an ice cream van and he loved to go to speedway at Poole. The earliest Christmas I can remember is my dad in a thick jumper and our sitting room being heated by one of those old free-standing paraffin heaters – a sort of cylinder shape.

When I was 5 we had another new arrival to the family – a baby sister this time, though it's so long ago I don't remember the arrival of my sister.

Another thing that stands out to me most in 1972, when I was 5, is being woken up in the middle of the night, and my family would get in my dad's old Ford Anglia and take a long Journey to London to stay at my grandma's for a while. I can specifically remember listening to Long Haired Lover from Liverpool being played most times when we went out in the Ford Anglia. It was a horrible car; I was always being travel sick in it.

Other groups I can remember hearing those days were ABBA, The Shadows, and Gary Glitter. We used to visit our uncle in Colchester as well, or he would come to my gran's to see us. My auntie would be there too, but she was more distant. My uncle was a fun-loving guy who I looked up to; I recall my uncle used to take us to London and Colchester Zoo.

The only thing I can recall about my mum in my younger days, is that she used to work in a pub. I think she was a cleaner and the pub was round the corner and down two streets away. She used to get me these nice mints wrapped in foil from the pub, and she would quite often bring home a tray of toffee and this little metal hammer that came with it for smashing it up.

I also recall I had a bedroom to myself, and when my dad had gone to work my mum would come and get me from my bedroom and let me get into bed with her for a cuddle. I also recall on many mornings I would be put off my breakfast as my mum would have dried up blood under her nose. I guess at that age it didn't really occur to me that my dad was beating my mum up the night before, it was just a horrible sight to see, when you're having jam on toast for breakfast.

At some age, I couldn't tell you if I was 5, 6, or 7, but my father used to wake up my brothers and I when all three of us were sharing a bedroom on the second floor. He would have come home from the pub, and tell me to get out of bed and lay on the bed face down with my pyjama top pulled up, then he would belt me with one of his three favourite belts for lashing us with. Then he would turn to my younger brother and do the same, but he hardly ever hit the oldest brother.

My dad's favourite belts were one which was leather with a black and white block pattern, a black leather belt with holes the size of 2p pieces, and his favourite of all was a reddish-brown short-haired belt with studs in.

We would get pulled out of bed for no reason at all, and thrashed time after time. It's not as if we were naughty kids, I mean, would you dare be naughty with a dad as brutal as ours? He was always drunk when he did it, it's only a shame his favourite pub, the Barley Mow, was around 200 feet from our house.

I guess I really woke up to life at about 7 years old, when my mum told us kids while my dad was at work, "I'm just popping to the shops, I'll be back soon."

But shortly after my mum left, my older sister gathered up my brothers and said, "I've got to take you to Mum's friend Joe's house as Mum has left for good and taken our youngest sister with her."

So we all went to Joe's house. It was a horrible house – they had a Dalmatian dog, the house was very smelly, and had a dark cellar. My sister left me and my brothers at Joe's while she went off to get my dad from work and tell him what had happened. My dad came to us a couple of hours later with my older sister and took us back home, and he told my sister to look after us while he popped out for a while.

Later that evening my dad returned with this lady and her four daughters who looked like they didn't have time to dress properly, arriving in just red tartan skirts and vests. One of the girls was 7, then there were twins aged about 5, and a younger girl, about 3. This was to be my new mother and sisters. That was quite a shell-shocking day. Not only did I lose a mum but I gained a mum and four sisters.

The home life got worse for us boys; we were told to stay out of the house all the time by our new mum. My younger brother and I spent many a freezing hour on the Green Croft in just shorts and tank top jumpers, being told to go out and play all day, but don't you dare get your clothes dirty. The Green Croft was a children's park just down the road from us, and very convenient for my dad, as he would still love to have his drink every weekend, and the pub the Barley Mow was conveniently set in our street opposite the park.

One evening when I had just turned 7, I walked down the stairs to the ground floor and as I reached the bottom step my legs just turned to jelly for no apparent reason, I just collapsed and could not feel anything from the waist down – it was a really scary moment. I can remember my dad carrying me down these long corridors at Odstock Hospital. I recall being left alone in bed at the hospital, and I desperately wanted to escape, but my legs were going nowhere. I recall while I was at the hospital the nurses wanted to give me an injection and I was having none of it. It took three or four nurses to hold me down, while I was given injections in my arms and in the back of my legs behind the knees. I recovered a few days later, and when I was 18 I was told I was treated for suspected Rheumatic Fever. All I could think of at 18, when I was reminded of this incident, is thanking

God I got my legs back because I sure enough needed them in the next few years.

My uncle from Colchester came to visit us occasionally and it was always nice to see him.

We had an evil uncle as well, he was as nasty as my dad could be. I recall this uncle in my house visiting once, and I had to play out in the garden and my mum was out shopping. I was looking through the back window; I kept peeping through to see if my mum had come home yet. He got really nasty with me and took me upstairs, and he laid on my mum and dad's bed, pulled me onto his chest, gripping my upper arms really tight, and with his evil eyes looking into mine, he kept demanding to know why I was looking through the window. He was nasty and scary, he would not except that I was just looking to see when my mum got home. I never told my mum what happened because it was no different than when for no reason, many times, my dad would pin my arms against the wall and taunt me about being called Steve. He would taunt me and say, "Why call yourself Steve when you have an 'E' on the end? You should call yourself Stevie." There was very little difference between my uncle and dad, so their behaviour towards me was just normal, and horrible.

When the stepfamily had settled in and I got used to the new ways of living, we used to get 10p pocket money a week. You could buy a lot of sweets for 10p and if my memory serves me well you could buy at least three sweets for a penny back then, my favourite being aniseed balls. All of us kids used to go to Saturday morning pictures at Salisbury Odeon. Those days we were given 12p; it would cost 10p to get into the Odeon and 2p to buy scraps of batter from Stobys Chip Shop on the way to the Odeon. The Odeon was open to children like a Saturday morning club – it was open 10am to 12pm, and you would get a raffle ticket for your 10p entry fee. Before we saw our regular dose of Thunderbirds, which I hated, and Cheeko the Rainmaker which I loved, there would be a draw to give a lucky kid tickets to see a real movie with a friend.

My younger brother and I used to spend a lot of time playing in four places; one was the council grounds next to the Green Croft – you could play hide and seek in the trees with your friends and end up in the occasional fight with other kids. We had been chased off the council grounds by kids with pen knives once, so one Saturday my brother and I went to the Saturday market in town and we stole ourselves pen knives to protect ourselves. We would also have to steal cold meat pies and sweets to get through the day at weekends, as we were not allowed in the house from breakfast to tea time. My stepmum's kids were not treated like that, they could come and go as they pleased.

My dad caught me and my younger brother with the pen knives one day and told us to pass them to him. I was petrified – I thought he would slit my throat with it. To my amazement he just handed them back and said, "Next time you steal something, make it worth your while in case you get caught; at least make it worth getting caught for."

I was gobsmacked.

My younger brother and I used to slip through a hole in the fence of a local brewery at the weekends and see if they had any leftover fizzy pop. That was in the days that the brewery would use Shire horses and a cart to deliver their beer around Salisbury – it was a lovely sight to see.

We used to go to a place called the flyover to go skateboarding with friends. The flyover was a new road that was being built, it was a bit of a slope with a wall at the top of it, one of Salisbury's planners' cock-ups; it was intended to take you from one side of the town to the other, and it was supposed to be built over the town, but planners got it wrong and the flyover was in fact heading straight towards Salisbury Cathedral. Needless to say they capped off the flyover when they realised the problem, and eventually turned that area into a multi-storey car park.

My first school was St Martin's infants; it was a small school set alongside the grounds of a church and graveyard. It was creepy there – I used to get the creeps when we had to go to that church. There's not a lot I remember about this school except the kids used to get free milk in these half-pint glass bottles, and we used to have a red barrel you could roll around the playground in, and on the way to school we used to be a little naughty and pinch milk bottles off people's doorsteps and drink the milk on the way to school.

When we stole food at the weekends to survive, we had the perfect hiding place at home. In the bedrooms on the top floor of the house, there were built-in chimneys, and inside the chimney there were metal plates that blocked off the chimney to stop a draught coming down. It was the perfect place to hide your goodies, you just lifted the flap and threw your goodies in there, then let the flap down again. It was at least two years before we got caught doing this.

I recall when I would wake up in the night, sometimes I would be really hungry so I would sneak down to the kitchen to find some food. One time I grabbed a dish and a pot of Bird's custard. I poured some custard powder in the bowl and added some tap water and to my horror, the custard set like concrete in the dish. I couldn't break the custard with my spoon so I opened the back kitchen door to the back yard which was a concrete floor and not thinking very smart, just panicking about how I was going to get the custard out the bowl, I threw the bowl face down onto the concrete floor. The bowl smashed into pieces and the custard stayed in a block, so I picked up the shattered bowl pieces and lump of custard and placed them into the bin in the yard – I got away with it. I also recall sneaking downstairs one night after my stepmum held a Tupperware party and I saw this bottle of drink called Warninks. It was thick yellow liquid, I thought it was banana milkshake so I tried some and I have to say to this day, that is the most disgusting drink I have ever tasted.

I suffered a lot with tonsillitis in those days, so when I was around 8 I returned to hospital, this time to have my tonsils removed. I remember taking my favourite teddy there, which was a golliwog in a suit. I recall Captain Pugwash was on the TV a lot back then, and I also recall a friend David from my infants' school was also on the same ward as me. I don't know if he was there for the same operation though. It was also nice after the operation because they give you ice cream as your first meal.

The night beating from my drunken dad carried on like normal.

My mum started to come through the Green Croft from the top to the bottom with our little sister. It was a bit uncomfortable seeing my mum come through the park, scared of what my dad would do to her or to us if he saw us talking to her; we had already been told, "If you see your mum, don't speak to her," so it was a horrible situation to be in. Anyway, we would go and speak to our mum and just hope we didn't get caught.

One time my dad bought some marshmallows and lit a fire in the back garden, and he was giving us kids toasted marshmallows. Then from the alleyway beside our house, our mum was softly calling us kids' names trying to get our attention. My dad looked at us all and put his finger over his mouth as if to say, "Be quiet, don't make a sound." He then sneaked back through the house and down the alleyway, and beat the living daylights out of my mum. It was horrific listening to my mum and baby sister both screaming their heads off.

Around the time my mum used to walk through the Green Croft I recall the firemen went on strike, and I watched the army in their Green Goddess fire engine putting out the fire of an overturned car at the top end of the Green Croft. This was also the time when on Escort Road, just round from the fire, you could buy a packet of 10 cigarettes from a vending machine on the wall in the street, so any kid of any age could buy cigarettes back then.

I moved up to St Martin's Juniors School; I quite liked that school, I used to be a very hungry boy and I recall every lunch time I used to eat all the kids' leftovers on my table, then I would have to go and sit on a bin against the wall and just sit back and watch all the other kids playing as I was too stuffed to move anywhere. We had a very strict maths teacher, she was a large woman and in her spare time she was a bell ringer. Her favourite pastime was, if you did not know your times table by a certain day, she would make you stand up and she would grab a clump of hair on top of your head and yank upwards for the amount of times tables you could not do. For example, if you could not do your 3 times tables she would yank your hair upwards 3 times. Well when it came to the 9 times tables I was really stuck. I went home from school knowing tomorrow I was going to get my hair yanked as I didn't have a clue how to do the 9 times table. Well, as life turned out I should be thanking this teacher, because I went to bed that night still not having a clue how to do the 9 times tables, getting ready for my hair-pulling session the next day, when by some miracle in the morning I woke up saying in my head *9, 18, 27, 36,* and so on. I had literally learnt the 9 times table in my sleep. It was an amazing feeling, and the reason I should thank that teacher is because ever since that day if I go to bed with a problem, I always have a solution by the time I wake up.

One of our favourite things we kids used to do together was go to the local swimming baths. It was an outdoor pool with a low roof above the changing rooms, so after a dip in the pool, which was always freezing, you could sunbathe on top of the changing rooms. They also had mangles for wringing out your swimming costumes.

Going back to the school, St Martin's Juniors, I do recall making friends with a girl called Dawn. All the kids used to pick on her and I didn't like what they were saying, so I made friends with her and we became good friends.

My mum was still coming through the Green Croft but she had now met a man she used to visit on Escort Road just above the Green Croft. He was a nice man; he owned a motorcycle shop. He made Harley-Davidsons and even owned his own racing bike – a Norton. He was always nice if we popped up to see him, always having little jokes with us, the perfect dad really.

\*

My dad did start to let us visit my mum and her new man when they lived on Wilton Road in Salisbury, but after a while they bought a house in Fordingbridge, 12 miles away from us.

The night time beatings carried on at home; sometimes my back would be bleeding from the lashings. My dad was no longer happy using the leather of the belt, instead he would use the belt buckles. Sometimes I would have to go to work with my stepmum. She worked in a local café called the Kadena. My back would be bleeding so bad, my stepmum would just pretend to the workers that I wasn't feeling well. Other times I would be taken to her friend's house four houses down, and she showed her friend my back, so sometimes the friend would look after me. Sometimes I was kept at home, but if any visitors came, I was hurried into a dark cupboard in the lounge, under the stairs, and told not to make a sound, or I would get hit.

I am now about 9 years old and I have been to visit my mum and stepdad in Fordingbridge a few times. I'd now become familiar with the 12-mile drive from Salisbury to Fordingbridge, so one morning, when I had had a good belt buckle lashing and my back was still bleeding from the night before, I decided enough is enough, I'm going to hitch hike to Fordingbridge and show my mum what my dad is doing to me.

I got to my mum's house and my stepdad was at work at the time. I showed her my back with cuts and dry blood from nights of lashings, and she said to me, "Your stepdad will be home soon and you must not show him your back, or he will go and beat your dad up and he'll end up in prison, and you wouldn't want that, would you?" So I agreed and when my stepdad came back my mum told him I had run away from my dad, but did not tell him why, so he took me back home.

I made many more attempts to get to my mum's after a good beating; sometimes social workers, just strange men to me, would pull over at the roadside and tell me to get in the car – they wanted to take me back home. Sometimes the police would pick me up and take me home. I was a frightened little boy, I never told the social workers or police why I was running away, I guess looking back now they must have just assumed I missed my mum, and that was the only reason I was running to my mum.

My dad and stepmum had made friends with these three horrible people, I didn't like them at all, they were always in our house, or we always had to go to their house.

One weekend my dad and stepmum decided they wanted to go away for the weekend and their three horrible friends would look after us, and further to this, my brothers and I were to stay shut in our bedroom all weekend with no food.

Well I woke up the Saturday morning and said to my brothers, "I am not staying shut in this bedroom with no food all weekend, we have done nothing wrong, I'm going to get dressed under the bed covers in case anyone comes up, then I'm going to get out on the roof and run away to mum and tell her."

I asked my brothers if they wanted to come but they were too scared, so I got dressed and climbed out onto the roof of this three-storey house. I climbed to the top of the roof so I could get along easier; at the end of the houses was a drop down to a garage with a flat roof, so I hung down and dropped onto the flat roof, then dropped to the ground and made my way to Fordingbridge.

The police caught me in Downton, 4 miles from Salisbury. This time they did not take me back to my dad; instead they took me to Salisbury Police Station. When we arrived at the station I was taken into a room where a sergeant sat down and talked to me. The sergeant said, "That was a very dangerous thing you did climbing out on the rooftops; you put my policemen's lives at risk going on the roof to search for you. Now I'm going to ask you a serious question, then this policeman is going to take you away for some lunch, then he'll bring you back and I want you to answer the question. Do you want to go back and live with your dad, or go and live with your mum, or go and live in a children's home?"

So I went for lunch. I already knew the answer, I wanted to go and live with my mum. So when lunch was over we went back to the sergeant, and I told him I wanted to go and live with my mum, so a while later my mum and stepdad came and collected me from the police station, and off I went to start my new life in Fordingbridge.

At this stage I am 9 years old and it's around September time.

We are now in 1976 – I have moved to Fordingbridge. My mum has had a baby and married my stepdad by this point, so in the house are my mum, stepdad, younger sister and half-brother, and myself. There was a Mickey Mouse clock in my bedroom and the ticking was soothing and used to send me to sleep. They had a lovely collie dog called Timber; the dog used to go round the bedrooms at night and quietly sneak onto the end of your bed, resting, like guarding you, but not sleeping. I had a small cottage-like bedroom window and when you woke up in the morning you could see the lovely garden and the field beyond. In the morning I was always woken by a cockerel in the neighbouring field, I used to love that sound.

I started a new school; it was very different to my old school. This school had soft cushion seats and large hexagonal tables, and the rooms were divided by sliding partition doors that run the length of the classrooms, so you could either divide the massive room into class rooms, or leave it as one big room. I made a friend there called Alistair and we used to hang around together after school.

Home life was so different. My stepdad was such a

kind person and always cracking jokes at the breakfast table; he used to sing along to the radio to songs like Reasons to be Cheerful, by Ian Dury, or Right Said Fred We'll Have a Cup of Tea Now, but I don't know who that was by. He never ever raised his voice to me and never hit me. I was so happy until one day I went to school and the children were saying that when you go to the next school they give you an injection and the needle is really big – I was petrified.

The next morning came and I was too scared to go back to school after the kids had said about the injections, so I stood outside the house. I couldn't tell my mum why I was upset and didn't want to go to school, because although my stepdad was nice all the time, my mum kept behaving funny with me. She would keep having a dig at me, saying, "Don't look like that, you look like your dad." It was like she was taunting me to get angry or upset. It was a horrible thing to say knowing what my dad had put me through, but she was always saying it when my stepdad wasn't around. So on this morning I was too afraid to go to school I just stood in the front garden and my mum was looking through the front lounge window, taunting me and pulling stupid faces at me. This time I was feeling really hurt and upset and she wasn't helping me by pulling stupid faces at me. I got so angry with her pulling stupid faces, that I picked up a lump of soil from the garden and threw it at the window at her as I was so cross.

To my misfortune there was a stone in the soil and I smashed the window, then I thought, *Oh no, my stepdad is going to be really angry with me now*, so I ran away. A social worker I had seen before picked me up and took me to a children's home in Downton called Paccombe House.

Before I go any further with my story I must go back about 6 months and remind you of the evil uncle who pinned me on his chest in the bedroom, and would not believe me when I told him I was looking through the window for my mum. Well about 6 months before I moved to Fordingbridge, I was going to the sweet shop around the corner with my brothers and sister and we bumped into my mum outside the sweetshop. My mum said, "Your grandma is dead. Your uncle used to go under her bed at night and frighten her. He stabbed your grandma to death." That was a shock, but I could believe it as I had already seen the evil side of this uncle for myself.

Now, back to Paccombe House Children's Home. I was taken into the home by my social worker and when I got there, it was a big home. I was introduced to a boy there and he was asked to show me around the home; the place was big and scary to me, all I wanted to do was run away, and after being shown around I took the first opportunity to get out and make a run for it. I wasn't running to anyone in particular, I just had to get away.

My social worker caught up with me about five minutes later and took me back to the home, so I resigned myself to my fate and decided, ok I won't run away, I will just see how it goes. In the evening I was sitting watching TV when I got a nice surprise – my stepdad had come to take me home. I was so relieved to see my stepdad and I apologised for breaking the window. I explained to him on the way back home that the kids at school had been talking about injections at the bigger school, and I was too scared to go to school, but mum was pulling faces at me in the window and I was cross with her, and I only meant to throw mud at the window. I didn't know there was a stone in it.

When we got home my stepdad told my mum what I said and she just laughed and said, "You silly boy, I was pulling faces to make you happy. I wanted you to be happy." I didn't say anything but it really didn't feel like that at the time, I was certain she was deliberately trying to wind me up.

I settled back down at school and continued to wander around with my friend Alistair, then one tea time, about mid-November, three large men came to our house to tell my stepdad and I that I would be put in a children's home. I do remember my stepdad pleading with them not to put me in a home before Christmas, but they said I would be going in a home in about three weeks' time. This is the first time I had heard these people introduce themselves as social workers, I did not know what social workers were before, but now in my eyes they were big, intimidating people who had come to take me from my home and put me in a children's home. I couldn't understand it. *I'm not a naughty kid, my dad's the bad man.* It was going through my head, *I'm going to a children's prison and I have done nothing wrong.* My mum made a point of telling me and my stepdad that it was my father's request that I be put in a children's home, but she didn't say that bit until the social workers had left.

# Chapter 2

## *Life in children's homes – age 9 to 16 years old*

Three weeks later a social worker came to take me to the children's home. We travelled a long way to this home, it was a place called Starfield in Trowbridge. I had never been to Trowbridge before; I was completely lost with a total stranger taking me away from my family.

When we arrived at Starfield there was a big car park and immediately to the left of it was this amazing set-up of three massive trees, with bridges joining the trees. It looked like a fun place to play. I was taken into the home and shown around by one of the staff. I was shown my bedroom, I was given some towels and bits, then I was taken down to meet the other children. These two kids called Milo and Jules took me under their wing, but they had planned to run away that afternoon and I had no choice but to go with them. It was scary. I didn't actually want to run away and I had no idea where we were going. Fortunately we were found by the police within an hour or so and we were taken back to the home.

Strange as it may seem, I was happy in the home and settled very quickly. The school I went to was a mobile classroom within the home grounds, so there was not a lot to unsettle me really, once I started to get to know the staff and kids, as all the kids, regardless of age, went to the mobile classroom for school, so it was very easy to get to know each other. In our spare time there was a games room that had a piano and a record player in it; I remember the most popular record played in the home was Puppet on a String by Sandy Shaw.

On Saturday it was pocket money day and the staff would drive us into Trowbridge and take us to the market to spend our pocket money. The best thing I can recall about our trips to Trowbridge market is, they were always playing Dancing Queen by ABBA in the market.

It was now Christmas time and I was allowed to go back and stay with my mum and stepdad for Christmas. It is a Christmas I will never forget. They had moved my half-brother into my old bedroom so I had a bed down in the sitting room under the window, overlooking the back garden. On Christmas Eve I woke up and I could not seem to breathe. I couldn't talk, I just felt panic as I tried to breathe. I went up to my mum's bedroom and she came to the bedroom doorway. She asked me what was wrong but I could not speak. My mum calmly took me downstairs and gave me cough medicine and told me I had croup. The cough medicine worked, I could breathe again, but it was a terrifying experience. My mum settled me back into bed and she went off to bed, but I could not sleep after such a scary moment, so I looked out the window and saw the most magical scene.

There was an outside light in the back garden by the kitchen's back door. It was snowing and there were three robins just hopping on and off the light onto the snow – it was Christmas morning and it was like magic watching the three robins just playfully hopping around. I forgot all about my croup, my heart was just filled with magic watching robins in the snow. I always send Christmas cards with robins on to everyone I love at Christmas, as robins mean something really special to me; I thought I was going to die that night and it ended so magically.

I can't say I really remember anything else about that Christmas; my birthday was on January 1$^{st}$ and I was now 10, and shortly after my birthday my stepdad and my mum took me back to Starfield.

There were two staff at Starfield called Peter; one of them had a very dodgy leg and walked awkwardly, but they were great, they used to take us for walks through the fields in the day or at night. I can especially remember loving the distinctive smell of the Tannery we used to pass on our walks. I had a close friend called Sean in the home, but he left and a pattern started to develop in my life. You would make friends with these kids and live with them like they were your brothers and sisters, only, you make a friend and try and be brotherly to them and the next thing is, they have been moved onto another home, you've lost a brother or sister, and in comes a new brother or sister to take their place. It took a bit of getting used to.

I made regular weekend visits to my mum and stepdad, but she did develop a habit of phoning up and cancelling my weekend visit on a Friday afternoon, the day I was due to go. She has no idea how hurtful that was or how upset I was every time she cancelled the weekends.

I was however, quite settled in the home though. I never felt like running away, we used have good meals, and I was well taken care of at the home. I recall we had a woodwork shop and the teacher showed us how to make a wooden fish, and it was the first thing I had made. I remember proudly giving it to my mum on one of my weekend visits.

I only had one bad experience with any of the children while I was at Starfield. That was when we went for our first weekly swimming lesson. Once a week this minibus, with wooden slatted seats, would come and pick us kids up, with a member of staff, and take us to the swimming baths. It was in my first swimming session; I was wearing arm bands as I could not swim. I was doing backstroke by the edge of the pool, when someone from behind me dunked my head underwater and held me there for a long time. I can't remember who it was now, it was either Milo or Jules, but I thought I was going to drown. I didn't do backstroke for a long time after that.

The only other bad experience I can recall at the home was, one morning I woke up for breakfast as normal and I was told I could not have breakfast as I was going to the dentist to have two wisdom teeth taken out. That was the first time I knew I was going to the dentist, so I was shocked to learn I was going to have two teeth taken out. Jane, a member of staff, took me in her car to the dentist. And I have to say that was the most disgusting and horrible experience to have. The dentist laid me in the dentist chair and said, "I am just going to put this gas mask over your face." I took a breath and inhaled the most disgusting smell – the only way I could describe the smell is that it smells pink. I hated the smell so much, that even when I was out cold, I can remember it like it was yesterday. When they gave me gas, I was fighting the dentist and his helper in my sleep, to get that mask off my face. I felt like I was fighting for my life, trying to get the mask off, but the harder I would try to get it off the harder the dentist would push it onto my face. In fact, I was out cold while I was dreaming this.

When I came around, the dentist said to me, "Which team won?"

I said, "What do you mean?"

He replied, "You were jumping around all over the place, like you were in a football match."

Then I threw up and continued to be sick in the car all the way back to Starfield. It was the most disgusting experience ever.

My social worker decided it would be a good idea for me to start spending weekends with my dad, stepmum and brothers and sisters, so I started weekend stays with them, and it was nice to see my brothers and sisters again.

I had been at Starfield for nearly 6 months now and I was very happy there, instead of bedtime beatings I would get bedtime stories. I recall the staff used to read us Mr Men books; it was a nice place to live, but all that was about to change.

My social worker came to visit me one day to explain that he was moving me to another children's home.

We are in 1977, and I'm 10 years old; this social worker is doing his best to explain to me as a 10-year-old, that I can't stay at this home because it's an assessment centre, and you can only stay in an assessment centre for a maximum of 6 months, so I have to be moved to another children's home.

So after settling down so well and no running away and no abuse, my world was about to be turned upside down, for no good reason in my eyes.

The time had now come to leave Starfield, but before we move on, it is important that I mention that within the first week of being placed into these children's homes, every child is seen by a doctor for a full medical health check, and I was no exception. This information will become relevant much later in the story.

Ok, so it was time to leave Starfield and go and spend the weekend at my dad's house, before being placed in this new children's home.

Monday morning comes and my social worker is now taking me to a place called St Margaret's Mead in Marlborough. This was approximately 28 miles from my dad's home, and 40 miles from my mum's home, and I had never been to Marlborough before. I really didn't want to move from Starfield, so going to this new home was really going against the grain inside me.

We are now in mid-1977. I arrive at St Margaret's Mead, and in comparison to Starfield, which was a large home set in its own surroundings, closed off to everyone like a big private home, St Margaret's Mead just looked like a normal house at the end of a row of houses, next to a park.

My first impression when I got inside the home was that it was a bit like a very large bungalow, only it had two floors. I recall one of the children was asked to show me where my bedroom was, so I could take my things up and unpack. When I got in the bedroom to unpack, some of the other children came in, and started going through my clothes and toys. I was very upset by this, and then the home manager came up to take me down to her office for a chat.

The one and only thing I can remember about that chat, is something that really went against the grain with me. She introduced herself as Ruth, and all the children called her Auntie Ruth and all the staff were to be called auntie or uncle. I was thinking to myself, *What a stupid idea. They're not related to me, why on earth would I want to call complete strangers auntie or uncle?*

I really didn't like the home and it is a stupid auntie and uncle rule, so the first opportunity I got I ran away. In fact for weeks just about every other day I would run away. Sometimes I would hitchhike to my mum's home, and sometimes I would hitchhike to my dad's. Lots of times I would not get all the way to either parent, as the police would catch me first and return me to the children's home.

In between the running away, I started at Marlborough Juniors School, where all the boys wore shorts as school uniform. I had had a medical check at the doctors, and I began to like the kids in the home, but still didn't like the auntie and uncle rule, and would not settle. It got to the point where I would just wake up in the morning, check the weather, and if it was a nice day, good, I will run away today, for no reason at all, I just liked running away more than I liked staying at the home – there didn't have to be a reason anymore.

My weekend visits to my mum dropped off considerably, but my weekend visits to my dad's increased a lot, and I was enjoying seeing my brother and sisters, including my stepsisters.

One of the girls at the home called Sophie and I had become very close and a bit experimental with each other's bodies, until we were caught in my bedroom in a very embarrassing position by one of the staff. Both Sophie and I were very embarrassed at being caught and we blamed each other, felt ashamed, and kept our distance after that, but we did get over our embarrassment and got along fine after a while.

One day, when I was returned to St Margaret's Mead from running away to my mum's, I recall having the most bizarre conversation with Auntie Ruth about me not liking wearing shorts at school. My mum had told her on the phone, I had run away because I didn't like wearing shorts to school, and before I could say no, she said a member of staff will take you to town and buy you a smart pair of trousers for school, so I thought, *Ok, I'm not going to argue, trousers are better than shorts anyway*. She asked if anything else was bothering me and I said, "Yes, I don't like calling the staff auntie and uncle, they are not my aunties or uncles," so she agreed I could now just call staff by their first name.

It was a bit weird now, calling all the staff by their first name, while all the rest of the kids were still calling them auntie or uncle. It didn't stop me running away though, I would just look out my bedroom in the morning and hear the birds chirping away, and to me it sounded like freedom, and that's what I wanted, freedom, so I would run away to be free like the birds. It was not an attention seeking thing, it was that feeling of freedom, to just get up and go and be free.

I hadn't been to the dentist since I was given gas to have my wisdom teeth removed, so I had to go to Marlborough dentist with one of the staff for a check-up. However, when I got in the dentist chair, it wasn't long before the dentist turned to me with a syringe with a needle in it, and said to me, "Would you like to inject yourself, or shall I do it?"

I was horrified. I replied, "But I'm only here for a check-up, what's that for?"

The dentist replied, "I have to give you two fillings."

I did not like that surprise. I leaped out of the chair and ran away, my faith in dentists now totally shattered by my gas experience in the last dentist, and this dentist asking me if I wanted to inject myself. When I was living in Salisbury I had no problem with my dentist, in fact I had had 7 fillings without an injection, but now I never wanted to see a dentist ever again, and I ran away to my dad's and was later returned to St Margaret's Mead.

By about October 1977, everyone was fed up with my running away, and they decided it would be a good idea to place me back with my dad.

So around November '77, while I am 10, I am returned to my dad, stepmum, and brothers and sisters, and I returned to St Martin's Juniors School.

There was no belting for a while, and I still felt uneasy with my dad, but I had stopped running away and started to settle. But after a while, my dad would return to his old ways and get out his belt.

My uncle from Colchester came down to Salisbury and took just me, for a holiday, back to his home in Colchester for a week.

On my first night at my uncle's, I was fast asleep and I felt someone shaking my right arm. As I was lying on my left side, I sort of stirred and looked over to my right, and saw this wavering black shadow looking over me. I turned back to go to sleep, then woke up in shock and thought, *What the hell was that?* I quickly looked over to my right-hand side, to see this wavering shadow appear to sink down into the floor and as it disappeared, I heard a loud bang. I then yelled out to my uncle and explained to him what I saw, and he let me go and sleep by the side of his and my auntie's bed for the rest of the week. Only on the return journey home, my uncle confirmed that the flat is actually haunted.

I had a lovely week at my uncle's. He took me to Colchester Zoo, and we bought two football mugs as presents for my brothers while we were there.

I got a bit naughty one day, because my dad had started belting me again, and I knew there was no point in running away to my mum anymore, as she would just keep sending me back for more beltings, so I thought, *I know what, I will ask my uncle to draw on a map, how we got to Colchester, then if I need to run away, I will run to him.* So I persuaded my uncle to draw the route we travelled on and give me the map to keep, so he did, but he didn't know why I really wanted it.

We are now into 1978, approximately April time, and I'm now 11.

My dad had given me one too many beatings for no reason at all, so the next morning, now that I had learnt the route to Colchester off by heart, I decided to run away to my uncle in Colchester, which was approximately 160 miles away. The distance did not bother me, I trusted my uncle, so off I went to find him.

I walked for about 3 miles out of Salisbury on the London Road, when I passed a layby on the left-hand side. I spotted an elderly couple in the layby. I could see they were just packing a flask away, so I thought, *When they pull out I will hitch a lift with them.*

The elderly couple pulled out in their brown Ford Cortina estate car. I stuck out my thumb, and they pulled over and invited me into the car. The old man said, "Where are you going?"

I paused for thought for a moment and realised, if I say I am going to my uncle's, he is not going to take me, so I replied, "I fell out with my dad who lives in Colchester and I ran away to my uncle in Salisbury. Now I'm trying to get back home."

The old man replied, "We live in London, so I will take you that far, ok?

I said thank you, and noticed this crate of chocolate éclairs beside me, and the old lady said, "Help yourself to a cake."

I felt like the luckiest boy alive. *I found an old couple who are really nice to take me to London, that's a big bit of my journey solved and all these lovely cakes to eat beside me, what could be better?*

On the approach to London I guess the old couple had taken a shine to me, as the old man looked over his shoulder to me, and said, "It's not safe to drop you off in London and let you find your own way, so I will take you home to your dad in Colchester and make sure you're safe. I couldn't believe my luck."

We arrived at my uncle's address and the kind old man knocked on the door, and when my uncle opened the door, the kind old man said, "HI, I have brought your son back home."

My uncle looked in disbelief and shock and said, "He's not my son, he's my nephew. You all better come inside."

My uncle sat me in the lounge, and then had a quiet chat with the old couple. When the old couple had left, my uncle said I was naughty to lie to the old couple, and that he has now got their name and address, and I must write a letter to the old couple and apologise for lying to them. The lovely couple's name was Mr and Mrs Snowdon. My uncle went on to say, "I will have to phone the police now and tell them you're here, and I will take you back home in a couple of days. Because of the confusion with me lying about who I was running to and from, the whole point of why I had run away had been lost and was never mentioned, and a couple of days later I was returned to my dad for more abuse.

Three days after I returned from Colchester, my brothers and I were asleep, when we were woken by four crying girls. It was what seemed like the middle of the night, and the girls, my stepsisters, came into our bedroom, crying and saying, "We are leaving now," and they turned around and left.

I couldn't believe it. I was thinking, *Oh no, this is all*

*my fault for running away to my uncle.* I felt terrible losing my stepmum and stepsisters this way.

I cried myself to sleep that night.

As the weeks went on there was just my dad, two brothers, my elder sister, and myself at home now, but my dad did find out my stepmum had taken her kids to live in a flat in the Friary, just 10 minutes' walk from where we lived, so we were allowed to visit them whenever we liked. I don't think my dad was much of a cook, as we seemed to be living on omelettes and nothing else.

I received a lovely letter back from Mr and Mrs Snowdon, and we stayed in touch for about four years; now and again, especially at Christmas, they would send me a little present, and sometimes I would phone them and have a nice long chat.

One day about three months down the line, around July 1978, I can't remember exactly what had made me unhappy, but my older sister and I were on the Green Croft. I said to my sister, "I'm going to run away to Mum."

My sister said, "Ok, I want to come with you, but I don't want to get in trouble," so she suggested she carry a lump of chalk, and put arrows on the path, to make it look like she was trying to show which way we had gone. So off we went, but after a while my sister turned back and I carried on alone. The best I can remember of what happened was, my mum sent me back to my dad's on the bus the next morning.

When I got home I was surprised to find my stepmum, and my stepsister, who was the same age as me, in our house. A couple of minutes later my dad walked into the house, and just started beating the living daylights out of my stepmum. My stepsister was screaming at me to help, and my stepmum was screaming as she was getting beaten up. I had to think quickly. *I thought, I know, I will get him to chase me. I will lock myself in the bathroom, I will climb out the little window, and run for help.* So I was standing near the top of the stairs, swearing at my dad and calling him every name under the sun. That got his attention and he ran up the stairs after me, and I escaped through the bathroom window, and I ran to Social Services two blocks away, and I demanded to be put back in a children's home.

My social worker spent a couple of hours trying to persuade me to go back to my dad, but I refused. I told him, "My dad beat up my stepmum and there is no way I will go back, I will just run away." I said, "You can even stick me back in St Margaret's Mead, and I'll even call them auntie and uncle, but I'm not going back to my dad."

My social worker finally gave in and took my dad and me to a children's home just on the edge of Salisbury, called Orchard House. When we arrived I was sent to the lounge, which was empty as the kids were at school, and my dad and social worker went off to the office with the home manager.

After a while, the home manager came and called me into his office, by this time my social worker had gone, and there was just my dad, the manager, and myself in the office.

As soon as I sat down, the manager started bawling and shouting at me and after about a minute he stopped and said, "Do you want to go home now?" I said no. I could tell he was surprised at my answer, so it was agreed I would stay at Orchard House. My dad left and I was left to roam around a bit.

When the kids came home from school, the first boy walked through the door, and stuck out his hand to shake my hand, and he said, "HI, my name is Jonathon, but you can call me John." I felt so at home after that.

Now I am 11 years old and it's 1978. I have a conscious decision to make at this point of the story, because I don't want this to turn into a kiss and tell story, but there are things coming up that you would not expect from a normal 11-year-old. Now it's probably best I explain that children in care are very confused about their feelings, so they may do things that are inappropriate for a normal child to do. But we were not normal children, we were either abused or neglected children and very misunderstood and incapable of talking through our abuse, or understanding who to trust or not to trust. Besides, this was not a normal home, parents with children, it was a home run by social workers, that can come and go as they please, quit the job whenever they wanted, so there was no real stability in our lives. Relationships between the kids and staff can be trusting one minute, then lost the next, as the staff move on. The relationships between the children are also different to your normal house hold, because you are now living with a few broken down children, who are now your brothers and sisters; they could leave the home and be moved on at any time, so it put relationships between the children under a lot of strain and very emotional or very aggressive, depending on how you were coping with your misfortune and how you were coping with your current environment.

I have decided to include inappropriate behaviour in the story, because it's true to life, this is what it's really like for kids in children's homes. It's not a kiss and tell story, it's fact. It's what life is like in children's homes and I was not the exception, it's just the way things are.

So back to Orchard House, when I moved there, it was only a week or two from school summer holidays, so I was not sent to school. Instead I was just left to settle in my new environment. I had a doctor's medical in the first week there.

I was about two years younger or more, than all the other children in the home, but the manager had a son he had adopted. He was about the same age as me, so we got on really well together, and I would spend most of my time playing with him. There were chickens and a couple of cockerels living in the grounds of the home, looked after by the gardener, so I was awoken by that nice sound of a cockerel again in the mornings, and I used to like going to collect the freshly laid eggs. The grounds to the side of the home were the size of a football pitch, with goal posts installed. They even had a moped for the kids to ride around the grounds, but when it ran out of petrol, one of the kids decided to fill the petrol tank with water, and that was the end of that moped. Also in the grounds was a mobile classroom, which we used for playing table tennis and darts. Beside the classroom was an outdoor swimming pool.

The manager of the home owned a caravan and in

the summer holidays he took some of us kids on a holiday.

I had become very fond of one of the girls; she was almost three years older than me, but very attractive with long blonde hair. Many times I would pop into the laundry room and other rooms to feel her breasts – I was in love. We never kissed or did anything else, just a quick feel every now and again.

It was now time to go to secondary school for the first time. Summer holidays were over and it was time to try and live a normal life. I was put in the bottom set at school with twelve other boys; I went to Highbury Secondary School in Laverstock, two bus rides away. I liked my new school and new friends, it was a comfortable size class for me.

There was this kid called Sean in the class, I had had a run in with him about three years earlier. I was going through this park called Churchill Gardens; I was riding my friend's bike and giving his little sister a ride on it, when this kid I didn't know jumped out from behind a tree and tried to whip us with a whip. I got off the bike, and gave the boy the thrashing of his life with the whip. I had the sense that I was acting like my father, so I stopped and rode off with my friend's sister.

I now learnt the boy's name was Sean and we were to be in the same class together. We instantly recognised each other and made friends, and became best friends throughout, secondary school. There was another friend too, called Andrew. I grew up sharing the same classes with him throughout my Infants' and Juniors' School, we also remained best friends throughout secondary school.

My mum had now moved with her family, to a place called Great Wishford – my stepdad had bought a cottage there, and he bought a big caravan for his family to live in while they knocked down the existing cottage to make two cottages. They had a little island as well, which they kept a cow, some ducks, and chickens on. I went to spend Christmas Day with them.

On Jan 1$^{st}$ 1979 I became 12 years old. I had settled in at Orchard House quite nicely, although there was the odd day I would get very emotional and sit on the stairs, take off my woollen jumpers and grab a thread and just pull the jumper to pieces. What was going through my mind at the time was, *Why am I in a prison for kids, when it was my dad that put me here and gave me all those hidings for nothing? Why am I in prison when I did nothing wrong? Why can't I live with my mum, and why isn't my dad in prison for what he did to me? It's all wrong. It's like I'm the guilty one and I'm being punished for what my dad did to me.*

I went through many jumpers with the same questions in my head.

There was a member of staff called Christine, she was just 21, a very nice lady who took us kids out for trips a lot, and every time we got in the car she would sing the song, With a Little Luck, by Paul McCartney. She had a very sad story; she had leukaemia and was only given two years left to live, so she was going to leave the home soon to get married and enjoy what was left of her life with her husband.

I could not swim and just used to go in the home swimming pool to splash around, but one day only I wanted to go in the pool, and Christine came to supervise me. I felt with Christine there I wanted to learn to swim properly, I had this deep feeling I wanted to make Christine feel like she had done something really good and helped me learn to swim. I wanted Christine to feel special. Someone called us for lunch and I was doing a hopeless job, but I could not give up, I really wanted to swim for Christine. I must do it for her. So I begged her for five minutes more, and to both of our relief I cracked it, I could swim and my swimming went from strength to strength, thanks to Christine, who after seeing how determined I was, booked me into Salisbury swimming baths for proper swimming lessons. A year later at school I got my bronze, silver and gold lifesaving badges and certificates. Christine had already died by then, of pneumonia, but she has never been forgotten as the one I really wanted to swim for.

Back to 1979. I am still having regular visits with my mum; she only lived 4 miles away, so I'd often walk there at the weekends, and my stepdad would take me back to the home later. Sometimes when I was feeling a bit screwed up, I would skip school and run away to my mum.

I was having a mixed up sort of relationship with a girl from the home called Sharon. She was a couple of years older than me, and we would quite often go up to Old Sarum and lie down in the woods, and I would feel her breasts. We were very close, we didn't do any more than that, it was just a shared bit of affection and lost emotions. This carried on until Sharon was moved on in mid-1979.

The home manager and his son also left the home around May 1979, and a new manager came in. I felt like I lost a best friend in the manager's son, but it was pretty normal really, kids and staff were coming and going all the time.

In the school holidays, I had fallen head over heels in love. The home manager hired a minibus and took all of us kids on holiday to a farmhouse. There were static caravans there, and a bar, and a sort of fun room for the kids. On the first night there, me and another boy from the home fell for two of the girls in the fun room. We listened to records with them all evening. The girl I fell for was called Cathy; I was 12 and she was 13. I was head over heels in love with this girl, and when it came to saying goodnight, Cathy gave me a full on French kiss – I was in seventh heaven after that.

My favourite record at the top of the charts was Bang Bang, by B. A. Robertson; it seemed very apt at the time. I discovered on holiday that I liked goat's milk, and whenever I drink goat's milk or here Bang Bang by B. A. Robertson, I can't help but remember my first proper kiss. Every evening I had a lovely time with Cathy. I also recall we had a lovely smooch to Hopelessly Devoted to You, from the Grease album. We didn't keep in touch after the holiday though.

It's now September 1979 and time to go back to school. I was very upset on the first day back at school, as they had moved me up two sets. I didn't know anyone and I couldn't understand anything I was being taught. I started to bunk off school as I hated the class they put me in. I would either hide in the town library for a while or run away to my mum. Eventually I was dropped down by one set, for lagging behind in lessons and not being able to catch up.

There was still no improvement in the next class, I was getting treated like an outsider and being bullied, so I carried on running away and bunking off school. I was getting so screwed up by then; I didn't know where I wanted to be.

In November that year we had new staff, a couple called Rob and Katie.

The first time I met Rob, I had run away to my mum and he caught me on the way and told me to get into the car. He drove me back towards Orchard House, but on the last bend, instead of turning right towards the home, he turned left and parked in front of the river. I was petrified. I seriously thought Rob was going to drown me in the river, my mind was so messed up. I started to cry with fear; he asked why I was crying, and I told him, "I'm scared you're going to drown me."

Rob calmed me down and said, "No, it's just a nice view, I thought it would relax you."

We talked for a while. I found a new friend in Rob and felt I could trust him, and then we went back to Orchard House.

In December 1979, the home manager organised a disco, to be held in our mobile classroom, and he invited Paccombe House Children's Home and Riverside Children's Home to bring their kids over to the disco.

At the disco there was a familiar face, it was Dawn, the girl everyone picked on at my Juniors School, but I went out of my way to be friends with. Dawn was with another girl and this other girl came up to me and said, "I'm Vickie, Dawn is my cousin over there and she asked me to ask you if you will go out with her."

So I said yes, and we danced and smooched the night away. We wrote to each other a few times after that, but we didn't see each other again.

I was still playing truant and lagging behind at school, so the school put me back down to the bottom set, back with my old friends, and in a class where I could understand what they were teaching us.

One day I skived off school with my younger brother and a friend and we went to Cathedral Close. There was a house that had a big aviary at the side. My brother was a bit of a bird lover, and didn't like to see the birds locked in a cage, so we set them free. The next day at school, we got the cane for it, six of the best, from the head master.

I spent Christmas day with my mum again.

It's now January 1980 and I'm now 13.

We went back to school, and I had got so used to bunking off most of last year, that I started to bunk off again. The home manager took me into the office one day after I bunked off school and said, "Ok, the running away and bunking off school stops now, or we will have no choice but to put you in a detention centre. The police don't want to be looking for you every day, so it stops now or you will definitely go to a detention centre."

So I agreed to stop. I was thinking in my head, *Why should I go to prison? It's my dad that should be locked up.* Anyway we talked about me joining a club, and agreed on first aid. So the next week, I joined the Red Cross in Salisbury.

At school after a few weeks of going to Red Cross, I told my brothers and friend about it. They liked the sound of it and joined the Red Cross as well; my brothers were still living with my dad, so to begin with, I would meet them at Red Cross as I had not seen my dad for a long time and I was scared to meet him.

I went on to have three successful years with the Red Cross; in April 1980 when I was 13 I got my first First Aid Certificate. In February 1981 I got my Youth Nursing Certificate and I also was awarded the shield for the most dedicated first aider in the Wiltshire region. You keep the shield for a year, and have your name engraved on it, then someone else wins it the next year. I am pleased to say my younger brother won the shield in 1983 and had his name engraved on it as well. The last I heard is the shield ended up on the wall in Red Cross House in Trowbridge, Wiltshire. In 1982 I got a certificate in January for Youth, Infant, and Child Care, and a Certificate for Elementary Junior Camping with the Red Cross.

So we are now back in January 1980 and I'm 13. There was a series on TV called Going Straight, starring Ronnie Barker. I remember after that chat with the home manager, about going to a detention centre, I made up my mind I was not going to run away or play truant anymore, and one day shortly after that chat, I sat in class and drew a big arrow, representing the arrows on a prison uniform, and drew it right across my big yellow folder. I wrote on top of the arrow 'I'm going straight', as a symbolic gesture to the teachers that I was going to behave from now on, just like Ronnie Barker.

I did break my 'being good' rule once though. All the boys thought it would be good if we all ran away together in the middle of the night; there were about eight of us, it seemed like a bit of a laugh, so we all got dressed and one of the boys' bedrooms had a fire escape leading off it, so we all escaped down the fire escape – it was about midnight when we left.

We started off by going through fields; as there were so many of us, it was a bit hard not to get noticed, but we ended up on the London Road, heading towards London. It was madness. Every time a car came, we had to dive in the hedges to avoid the police. This had to be the slowest escape ever, because the police caught up with us about 3 miles out of Salisbury on the London Road, at about 6am. The police got out of the car and ran full speed towards us. I was the youngest and smallest. Everyone ran off as fast as they could, but a policeman caught me, and was holding his truncheon above my head, shouting, "Everybody stop!"

Well it had the desired effect; all the boys came back and gave up. We were all taken back to the home and lined up in the corridor, each waiting to go in the office and get a rocket, from the home manager. By time I got in the office the older boys had stuck up for me and said, "Don't punish Steve, it was our idea, he just felt he had to come along." So although the others got punishments for a month, they made sure I got off.

A similar thing happened about a month later. The boys slept four to each bedroom and there were two bedrooms, and about half an hour after we all went to bed, the boys from the other bedroom came into our room and started a food fight. They were throwing just about everything imaginable, eggs, flower, flans, tomatoes, everything went crazy for a good 20 minutes, then a member of staff came up, and again we were all lined up outside the office, waiting for an ear bashing from the manager, and again the older boys took the blame and said it had nothing to do with me, and I was let off punishments again.

While I'm on the subject of being a little naughty from time to time, we used to have some good pillow fights against the other bedroom. I recall sometimes, we would scatter drawing pins on the floor near the door, so when they came charging in, they got a foot full of drawing pins – that was fun.

There were a couple of twin girls in the home. I had a strange experience with one of the twins once. I had come in the back door and walked into the dining room up to the kitchen hatch, meanwhile Julie, one of the twins, walked down the hallway into the kitchen and up to the hatch, and we both just leaned over and gave each other a big kiss on the lips. From then on, when we had cigarette breaks together I would fondle her breasts – she was a soft, gentle girl.

Rob and Katie were my favourite staff there; they were a young, energetic couple. Rob owned a Ducati Pantah 900cc motor bike, which he used to take us kids out on. He had a Jawa before that, and Katie had a Moto Guzzi 500cc, and they had a Sunbeam car as well. Rob was a very clever, intelligent man and very smart too; he knew how to engage with the kids, he would teach us never to lie, and how to keep the right side of the law. Rob also had a sailing boat in Poole and would quite often take two or three kids for a trip on his yacht, up to the Isle of Wight and back. He used to have the Band on the Run album by Paul McCartney on the boat, so if I hear a song from that album it always reminds me of our sailing days.

I had a crush on this new girl that came in, she was a couple of years older than me. I used to sneak up to the girls' bedroom and sit on her bed and talk to her, but I never quite had the guts to ask her out or tell her I fancied her.

In May 1980, Starfield, my old children's home in Trowbridge was holding a sponsored Le Mans Walking Race, which was basically where you have teams of two people, and the sponsored walk was 12 hours long. One person walks or runs round this half-mile course, while the other person rests, and you just take turns in doing as many laps as you want then swapping over. You wore a number on your front and an arm band when you were the runner, and there would be people sitting at a desk on the route, keeping track of your team's laps. It was so nice to go back and see my old home. By the end of the day, John and I achieved 60 miles over the 12 hours, so we were very pleased with ourselves.

In the summer holidays, Rob and another member of staff took us on a camping holiday in the New Forest; it was nice waking up to deer outside your tent first thing in the morning.

I recall I got a bit naughty and cheeky one day, but I was soon put in my place. The new member of staff was a very overweight guy, and I rather stupidly started taunting him, while he was just sitting drinking his black tea. I was saying, "Come on fatty, catch me. You're too fat to catch me." I kept saying it, and the guy just lost his rag and threw his black hot tea straight over me. Well, it taught me not to be so rude to anyone again.

I was still having the occasional visit to my mum's, and on Tuesday nights I would now go to my dad's house to meet my brothers to go to first aid.

My younger brother gave me £10 one day – he said he had stolen it from a shop till, where he was friends with the shop owner's son. I didn't want or need the money, but I understood that my younger brother was stealing the money to buy food to survive, as he was not getting enough food at home, so I could not say no to taking the money, as I didn't want to hurt his feelings. If we were living together we would have shared it. The next day I took the money to school, then spent it after school, but I didn't really need anything, so I bought a skateboard and a first aid kit, and hid them under my bed when I got back to the home. John saw me stash the things under the bed and told Rob about the stuff, thinking I stole them, so I had to come clean to Rob. Rob called the police, and around September '80, my two brothers and I ended up in court as my younger brother had been stealing from the till for quite a while. We all got a court order to stay in care until we were 18, and my two brothers were put in Riverside Assessment Centre in Salisbury, until suitable children's homes were found for them.

About four weeks after my brothers were put in care, I came home from school to find the home manager waiting in the car park for me. He said, "Your dad has been sexually abusing your sister and has been sent to prison, and your sister is in a hostel."

He also said the police wanted to question me. "But I told them no, they can't question you, because you were no longer living with your dad, and would not know anything about it." So that's how things were left, except I now thought my dad was even sicker in the head than ever, and I felt sorry for my sister.

My social worker went on to arrange prison visits, for my brothers and I to go and visit Dad in prison. I could never understand why the social worker was taking me, because as far as I was concerned my dad was a sick bloke and I would be happy never to see him ever again, but they kept taking me. I had nothing but disgust for him.

On a lighter note, at the weekends I would spend a lot of time with a friend from my class called Mikel I'd go over to his house a lot. I had a bit of a soft spot for his younger sister Stephanie. She was a sweet, skinny girl, so I always called her fatty, with a bit of affection.

When I finally found out where my sister was living, I went to visit her and she explained that my dad had been sexually abusing her since she was about 4 years old. I was horrified for my sister and we became very close after that, and I would pop in and see her frequently.

It's now Christmas 1980 and I went to spend the day with my mum again.

It's now January 1981 I'm now 14. I had stopped running away for quite some time. I loved school. I forgot to mention, that I gave into peer pressure in the home and started smoking at the age of 12.

We used to get 50p lunch money each day, so on

the way to school, I would pop to the shop and buy 10 cigarettes which cost about 45p. I loved my Embassy number 1s, my social worker used to smoke them too. At lunch time I would go out of school with my best mate Sean, and we'd have a smoke on the way to this little bakery about 10 minutes away from the school. The bakery was great, they sold day-old jam doughnuts for a penny and day old lardy cakes for 2p, and Sean and I spent the rest of our school life buying a packet of cigarettes a day and cakes for lunch.

Sean and I hated art, so every art lesson we would go to the sports hall together and fix table tennis bats. The Deputy Head was always on the warpath looking for people bunking out on lessons, and quite often stopped us on the way to the sports hall.

I was disgusted to learn, my dad only got 2 years for all those years of sexual abuse to my sister, and I was disgusted and angry, that he didn't get any time for all the abuse he put me through.

My younger brother came to live with me at Orchard House, and my older brother was moved to Paccombe House Children's Home in Downton.

I remember one day I had some spare change on me, so on my way home, I went into the record shop and bought my favourite record out at the time, which was Drowning in Berlin by the Mobiles. I went out the shop with it, and realised I would be the laughing stock of the home if I went back with this record, so I went back and changed it for Big in Japan by Alphaville.

In May it was time to go back to Starfield to do the

Le Mans Walk again; this time I did it with my younger brother. It was nice to do this together, and at the end of the day we beat last year's results of 60 miles that John and I did – this year we got 63.5 miles.

We were both still making the occasional visit to see Mum.

We used to pop over to Paccombe house and visit my older brother too, and the prison visits continued as well.

My younger brother, for some unknown reason, was moved from Orchard House to Hillside Children's Home, in Warminster, Wiltshire.

It's now summer holidays 1981 and Rob plans to take four of us kids in his yacht to France.

I was really looking forward to this holiday. We arrived in Poole about 4pm and had a big meal in a café as Rob said you shouldn't sail long-distance on an empty stomach. We had passed the Isle of Wight by 7.30-8pm and we all took turns at steering the yacht. At midnight I was tired and went down into the cabin to sleep. I woke up at 6am and felt really awful, so I went on deck and was constantly throwing up over the side of the yacht. After about an hour of throwing up, one of the lads shouted, "There's the Isle of Wight!"

I said, "What do you mean the Isle of Wight? We passed that last night."

Then Rob said, "The sea got too rough and we had to turn around."

I thought, *Oh no, I just have to get off this boat and don't want to go to France if I'm going to be ill like this.* So when we pulled into the Isle of Wight, I asked Rob for some spending money. I then went straight to the ferry ticket office, bought a ticket home and made my own way back to Orchard House. I did get in trouble, as they were all searching for me on the Isle of Wight; I was just happy to be home and off the yacht, sea sickness is awful.

Apart from going to First Aid, I started going to City Hall discos and meeting up with my classmates. We all became what was known back then as rude boys, wearing green flight jackets and Doc Marten boots, there was about 9 out of 12 kids in our class that became rude boys and we liked groups like, Madness, Bad Manners, and all Ska music.

I started spending the occasional weekend at Hillside with my younger brother, just so we could spend some time together.

It's now Christmas '81 and I spent the day with my mum again.

We are now into January 1982 and I am 15, and I am allowed to start visiting my uncle in Colchester. I was to catch a coach from Salisbury to London Victoria Station, then switch coaches to Colchester. I used to travel up on my own on Fridays and meet my uncle at the coach station his end, then he'd take me back to the coach station on Monday mornings. We used to do this about every three weeks.

We also discussed at the home, about the possibility of me being fostered, and took a photo of me to go into the fostering file; I still have a copy of that photo today.

In February my older brother invited me over to

Paccombe House as they were holding a Valentine's Disco. I really liked a girl who spent all evening standing near the disco lights but never danced, I did not have the courage to walk over and ask her out, so after the disco I asked my brother what the girl's name was, and he said, "Her name is Ellen and she's the boss's daughter."

When I got back to Orchard House I wrote a letter to Ellen and asked her out. A few days later I got a reply from Ellen saying yes, she would go out with me, and we exchanged letters for about three weeks. Then I got this letter from Ellen saying, "Sorry but my dad said I can't go out with you because you live in a children's home."

I was very upset, but there was nothing I could do.

I was still doing regular trips to the prison, I couldn't stand my dad, but it was a day off school so what the hell. I was enjoying school though, and I was still making the occasional visit to my mum and to my younger brother.

My sister did not like living in the hostel so she bought a tent and camped on the camp site at Hudson's Field, just round the corner from Orchard House, so I saw her more often as well.

Around April, my social worker said my uncle in Colchester would like to foster me, so we are working on that.

In May my older brother told me Dawn's cousin Jackie would like to go out with me, so I said yes, and went over to Paccombe House to see her. The trouble is, a couple of girls, one of them being Ellen, who I really liked but couldn't go out with, came to join us on the front lawn. I fancied Ellen a lot and felt uncomfortable dating Jackie, in front of Ellen, so I went off to find my brother and told him, "I'm going home," and I didn't go out with Jackie after all.

My younger brother got fostered and moved to Tisbury to be with his foster family.

My older Brother left Paccombe House to live with a lady that used to be their house cleaner to help my dad out. I got to know this lady and she used to work in a china shop in town, and some Saturdays I used to go in and help her sell the china.

Apart from going to City Hall discos and First Aid, I started to go to City Hall to watch the live wrestling every other week – I loved it. Occasionally I would also pop over to Victoria Park to watch Salisbury Football Club play.

In May '82 my social Worker told me my uncle from Colchester had pulled out of the fostering. I was very upset; I stopped going to his house and I packed in First Aid as well, I couldn't see the point in doing good for others if that's the way I was going to be treated.

One day I went to visit my younger brother and his foster family – they were a very nice family. Just before I left their daughter Ann Marie came into the lounge, she was the same age as me, with blonde hair and blue eyes. I was in love from the moment I saw her, but it was time to leave, so I wrote to her and asked her out, and Ann Marie replied yes, so unfortunately for my younger brother I was so head over heels in love with Ann Marie, that when I was supposed to be going over to see my younger brother,

I was actually going out for long walks with Ann Marie. We would go to a place called Wardour Castle, and stop in the woods along the way to make love. We would also make love every Friday, when I bunked off college I would spend the day with Ann Marie at her home instead. Ann Marie gave me a photo that I used to carry with me everywhere and proudly show her off to all my friends at school.

One Saturday Rob took me in his car down to Poole to fix the lining in his yacht. We were using Evo-Stik, to stick up the lining and after a while we came out the yacht for some coffee. Rob said something quite normal to me and I just burst out laughing, then he started laughing, then neither of us could stop laughing for a good ten minutes; we were as high as a kite on Evo-Stik.

Just before the summer holidays Rob bought a kit car called a Marlin that needed to be built from scratch, so Rob and I spent the whole summer holidays building the Marlin and his wife made all the upholstery. I had a great summer building the car and popping off at the weekends to see my younger brother and Ann Marie.

I was now in my final year of school. September '82, I started to go to Salisbury College on Fridays, as day release from school, and I opted for the building course. I would be taught plumbing, brick laying, carpentry, and painting and decorating.

After going to college for the four weeks and doing my best at everything, I was fed up of listening to the brick laying teacher saying to the same couple of boys, "Your dad bought me a drink last night, I'm marking your work down as an A." This same teacher did the same thing four weeks in a row and I was fuming because I didn't have a dad to buy him a drink, so if that's the way we're being graded I might just as well not bother coming, at all. So on Fridays instead of going to college, I would catch a train to Tisbury and spend a long weekend with my brother's foster family, to spend extra time with Ann Marie in bed or in the woods if at all possible.

Rob had stopped working at Orchard House and gone on a college course full time.

I went to Wales for a week in October, with the school, to a mountaineering rescue centre, and towards the end of the week, we did a canoeing skills challenge, and later after we returned to school I received a Welsh 1 Star canoeing certificate and badge, which I still have today.

This year I spent Christmas Day with my brother's foster parents.

January the 1$^{st}$ is here again and I'm now 16.

Time to go back to school. My entire life has now changed for the better, I go to school four days a week then have a three-day weekend at Tisbury, with my girlfriend Ann Marie, and I get on so well with the family, so much so that they start to ask me what I am going to do when I leave school and where I am going to live, because they would like to foster me.

Around March time, my girlfriend's parents, my social worker, the home manager, and myself, sat down and had a chat about me being fostered. I proposed that I be taken in as a lodger rather than a foster child, because I felt more comfortable that way. I felt I was too old to be fostered, so it was agreed by all to take me in as a lodger once all the paperwork was completed and I had finished my school exams. In the meantime I carried on with the weekend visits and Ann Marie and I were still very much in love.

Dawn, the girl I made friends with at junior school, came to live at Orchard House. My exams were finished and I was ready to leave school and move to the foster family, when the home manager called me into the office one evening and said, "We need to have a chat. There is one condition to you moving to Tisbury, you must stop seeing Ann Marie."

I said, "No, I can't do that, I won't go and live there then," and I left the office.

I walked round for four or five days mulling things over. I was thinking, *My exam results are going to be really bad and I only took two exams. How am I ever going to get a job with bad results and a kids home for my address?* I didn't stand a chance. *And what about the foster parents? Are they going to let me see their daughter if I turn down going to live with them?*

I realised whatever I did I had lost Ann Marie either way. So I went back to the manager and said, "Ok, I accept the terms. I don't seem to have any other choice."

After that, I made love with Dawn a few times, because I was devastated about losing Ann Marie, and Dawn was a nice girl and I was at the point of 'what the hell?' I'd lost what matters most so why should I care anyway?

Ellen from Paccombe House phoned up out of the blue, and said her mum had now left her dad, and it wasn't her real dad anyway, so she would like to stay in touch with me if that was ok. I said yes and we left it at that for now.

So I moved to Tisbury with the family, and it was clear Ann Marie wanted to carry on the relationship, but if I allowed it to continue I would have just been put back in Orchard House. I couldn't win. Then I spotted the next-door neighbour, a girl the same age as me. *Perhaps if I ask her out, Ann Marie will turn to hate me, and the problem would be solved.* So I started hanging around with the girl next door. I liked her but not in the same way as Ann Marie, although I did feel her breasts and play around down below, whilst sitting in the garden one day. I could tell the neighbour wanted to make love. When we were walking next to a wheat field one day, we rolled around in the wheat but it wasn't really her I wanted to be with, it was Ann Marie, so I pretended I did not know what she wanted.

Ann Marie started fighting with her mum, and it was awful to see Ann Marie getting in such a state. I was beginning to feel guilty, because I wasn't doing anything with the girl next door, I was just using her to make Ann Marie jealous enough to hate me, so that I didn't end up back in Orchard House. I didn't really want to hurt her at all, I just had to.

One day Ann Marie had such a big row that her mum got her a room above the local pub, and Ann Marie was effectively kicked out. I felt awful about the whole thing, but it was all too late. The damage had been done; there was nothing I could do to put it right.

# Chapter 3

## *My colourful career started on the Rodeo Switchback*

In December 1983, my foster mum's mum, took me to a place called Stainers in Fovant. She wanted to show me this old fairground ride, owned by a company called Switchback Ventures Ltd. The company had an old ride called Rodeo Switchback, which they had just brought back from America, where it was going to be burnt. Switchback Ventures Ltd was formed by five men who had their own businesses and wanted to jointly save this ride as the oldest merry go round that would be travelling today once up and running, and the only one of its kind left in the world. They were holding the open day to try and attract shareholders. The ride was being stored at Stainers. As for the restoration, it would require a lot of room to store this ride and move bits around whilst restoring it.

On the open day, there was a steam engine running Anderton and Rowland's fairground organ, and a big timber frame measuring approximately 50 feet across – it was a round ride with two hills. The ride was in such poor condition they could only put up the framework and the tracks that the cars would sit on and the roof. The cars, figureheads, railings and centre truck, and other bits were stored in every space available in Stainers, which was actually a large mechanics garage, where they repaired military vehicles.

My foster mum's mum was somehow related to one of the company's directors and she got me a job interview with the company. I had my interview in the pub in Fovant, and was offered a job on the youth training scheme, to help restore the ride. So I started work for Switchback Ventures Ltd in December '83.

I was shown on my first day how to use a gas naked flame to burn the paint off the hand railings. The railings had very intricate carving on them, and it would take me two and a half days to burn the paint off one side of each section of railings. It was an amazing room to work in, being surrounded by all kinds of figureheads like cowboys and Indians, bears, a mermaid, Harold Lloyd, and many, many more. The cars also had amazing carved patterns and figure heads on them; a lot of the paintwork contained gold leaf, but it all had to be burnt off, to see what kind of condition everything was in under the paintwork. My boss's wife was working on burning the paint off the more intricate figureheads.

Elsewhere in the mechanics garage, there was a guy restoring the cheese wheel, which was the bit on the centre truck chimney that turned and pulled the roof around, which pulled the whole ride round. There was another guy called Tony, who worked with someone else to make new trailers to carry the ride around on. Tony also made sleeping quarters at the end of one of the trailers that would carry some of the ride.

By time the trailers were completed, when we did go on tour, there were two loads to be pulled. It took five trailers to carry the complete ride, both loads being just over 100 feet long.

In the week I started, the local news had come along to talk about this old ride, and let the public know the company was looking for shareholders to help restore the ride and get it back on the road. So for the next few days in the village, I had people coming up to me saying, "I saw you on TV on the news." I missed it myself.

Well, Christmas came and went. My birthday was on Jan 1$^{st}$, I am now 17 and I have a brilliant job restoring the ride; I loved every day of my work life.

In January I popped into Salisbury, into town, and bumped into a girl I used to live with at Orchard House – her name was Sarah. We arranged to meet up some other time and go to the pictures, so we met up and went to the pictures, then we went back to my foster home. No one was in, so Sarah and I made love in my bedroom, then she went back to Orchard House. I did not want a serious relationship and Sarah did, we got our wires crossed, but we sorted it out and remained friends.

During lunch breaks at work I used to go and have lunch with the mechanics, who worked on the military vehicles. Two of the mechanics were father and son; they both owned cars used for banger racing, but these cars were built more like dune buggies. The mechanics would work on the cars through their lunch breaks, to get them ready for the next season's racing. I started going to race meets with the son as we got on really well.

In April '84, the mechanic's son and I went down to Orchard House to visit Rob and Katie. The mechanic's son and Rob got chatting about banger racing, and Rob got really interested in buying one of these dune buggy like cars and coming to a race. Rob said he had too many cars and offered me his Ford Anglia for £50, so I bought it and got it taken back home to Tisbury. It just sat on the drive for a while, as I couldn't drive, and working for a fairground company I could not afford the insurance to learn to drive.

Rob had bought his racing car and brought it to the race meet, and he flipped it on to its roof in his first race – he didn't come racing again after that.

In May my next-door neighbour came to see me about the Ford Anglia. He said, "Would you sell it to me for £30 plus a moped?"

So I said, "Yes, ok."

I got my insurance and helmet and I was finally mobile, it was great to get out and about wherever I liked now, and no more cycling to work.

It's now June and I was pining to ask Ann Marie out again, so I asked her out and she said yes, but she didn't seem very happy about it. It was more like she was still hurting from what I did to her. I felt wracked with guilt and thought, *This can't work, it's as if I had done something so bad Ann Marie could never forgive me.* I felt so guilty the only thing I could think of was to say to her, "My mechanic friend is nice and he likes you and he is single, would you like me to see if he will go out for a drink with you?" So I put it to Ann Marie and she said ok, so I fixed them up on a date.

Shortly after that, the mechanic would not hang around with me anymore. He said, "Ann Marie does not like me hanging around with you," so I got the feeling Ann Marie was still mad at me, although at the time, I couldn't think what else to do for the best. I spent years writing apology letters to Ann Marie, about what I had done to her, but she would never reply or except my apology.

July '84 and we're getting all the final touches done on the Switchback, ready for its grand opening at Stourpaine, next month.

August is upon us and it's time to go to Stourpaine.

We had two loads at 100 feet long; it was amazing to see all that was just one ride, and we had never seen it all put together before, so this was going to be a really special build up, watching the jigsaw coming together after burning off paint for months and re-painting everything. The boss's wife had done some excellent marble painting on everything, you just knew this ride would look impressive once it was built.

We were building up next to the dodgems, which belonged to a company called Cole's Fair – they used to own a Switchback, but not the spinning top kind, theirs had a static roof and was now in a museum, but they knew how to build a Switchback, so they were just as interested to see this ride built as we were. There were about seven of us building the switchback and it took about two and a half days to build the ride, but it looked impressive once built.

We held a private opening for the press and to test the ride out. It would take 64 passengers to fill the ride, and the ride was full of passengers. The roof started creaking as it took up the weight and gently the ride would start to go round, so the boss sped it up, when, the all of a sudden, the back end of one car and the front of the connecting car derailed. It was an awful feeling; my heart was in my throat. All the Switchback staff just froze, all our work just broken before us. I just wanted to hide under something. The ride was full and cameras were everywhere, I just wanted the ground to swallow me up, it was awful. The next thing I saw the Cole's brothers run towards the ride with some of their workers, and they just picked up the cars and threw them back on the track.

The reason the cars came off, was because all the rods coming down from the roof to the connections to the cars, were only connected by hooks, and one of the hooks disconnected and the rod buckled up and forced the cars off the track. To prevent this happening again, D shackles were fitted where the hooks were, and thankfully the second test run went smoothly, as did the rest of the week.

September was exciting as we were going to take the ride to Salisbury, my home town. I was so proud working on the Switchback, I couldn't think of a better place to take the ride. The build-up was absolutely incredible; it took seven of us two and a half days to build the ride at Stourpaine, in Salisbury the ride had to be built in just one afternoon, to be ready to open by 10am the next morning. Once again, the Cole's brothers and all their crew were on hand to help us. It was manic; there were men everywhere bits and pieces flying up all over the place, but it was built by 10pm that night – it was incredible.

After Salisbury fair, we didn't go anywhere else this year, but carried on restoring the ride throughout the winter to get ready for the next year's touring season.

In October I got a phone call out the blue from Ellen, the girl I knew at the children's home, the manager's daughter at Paccombe House. Ellen had got my phone number from Orchard House. Ellen had phoned me up to see if I would like to go to her house to see her, so I said yes.

When I got to Ellen's one evening, I got a bit of a surprise; she had cut all her hair off, and as the evening went on, I learned that Ellen had spent a lot of time in India and was well into Buddhism, something I had never heard of before, and her house reflected furnishings of a Buddhist believer. It was a lot to absorb. I'd never come across a girl like this before, especially with such deep-rooted religious beliefs. I kept visiting Ellen through October and November; we did kiss goodbye every time we met, but nothing more, as we never quite connected. I was very fond of her and interested in what Ellen had come to believe in, but we never quite made a connection. I recall we went to the pictures in Salisbury once to see Karate Kid, and I was impressed with this film, because Ellen had been explaining to me about her Yin Yang badge and what it meant, and this film came over in the same way. I thought it was very clever and Ellen made me look at life in a totally different way, as did the film.

Ellen invited me over for tea one night and said

that she was going to cook for me, but when I went for tea that night, halfway through cooking the tea, Ellen started to cry and asked me to leave. I couldn't get Ellen to tell me what was wrong, so I left. It was strange that night, because the moon was lit so bright, I could almost see all the way home, without needing lights on my moped.

Christmas came and went, and then it was my $18^{th}$ birthday. I did not go to pubs, I guess in the back of my mind I just associated pubs with drunken violence, thanks to my dad. I did get a bottle of wine from my foster parents, so I spent all afternoon drinking red wine. When it came to about 6pm I was not drunk in the slightest, but the foster mum shouted, "Tea time!" and I just threw up, and went and lay down on my bed. The room was spinning. I decided I wouldn't bother doing that again, there was nothing nice about it and since then I have never drunk more than three pints of lager, partly because I didn't enjoy or see the point of the after effects of getting drunk, and partly because I didn't want to turn out as a drunken thug like my dad.

It's now march 1985 and it's time to tour around the country with the Switchback.

Occasionally I would drop a line to Ellen and tell her how things were going, but I never got any replies.

Some of the places we toured to were a bit memorable, like Shepton Mallet, where we built up outside a large furniture store. We were there to help promote the store; all visitors to the store would get a free ride on the Switchback. We went up to Granada Studios to do filming for a film called Lost Empires. While we were at Granada Studios, we were also shown around the Coronation Street set, and I sat in the audience on one of the Krypton Factor shows, whilst it was being filmed. The Lost Empires filming meant we had to dress up in really old clothes, I think from the around the early 1900s. I was paid an extra £100 that week, as an extra with technical skills, so that was a nice bonus on top of everything else. From there we went on to a steam rally and saw the best set of Gallopers I had ever seen, owned by James Noyce. They were immaculate. The owner would let his Rottweiler sit in the middle of the ride, and it would quite often go round the centre truck and follow the ride around.

One steam rally we went to was on the outskirts of a little village. On the first day we opened the ride we heard a tremendous roaring sound coming into the village, it turned out to be approximately 80 or so Hell's Angels turning up on their bikes for their annual meet at the fair. Another time we went to Bristol and the Mods turned up in vast numbers on their Lambrettas, for their annual meet at the fair. We went to many fairgrounds and steam rallies in between, but these were the most memorable.

We finished the tour at Stourpaine this year, and the company could not afford to keep us on in the winter, so my boss asked me to come back in March next year and bring a friend as we needed another crew member. If you can imagine most fairground rides can be built in two or three hours by a crew of four people, with our crew of six it would take two and a half days to build the ride and a whole day to pack it all away again, so basically in any seven days we would spend three and a half days of that either building up or pulling down the ride, so most times we stayed at places for up to two weeks, or thereabouts, if possible.

I sold my moped towards the end of the tour and bought a 50cc black Honda with five gears; I seemed to get an extra ten miles an hour out of that, which was fun.

My older brother now lived in Scotland, working as a mechanic. He got in touch with me and asked me to come up and live in Scotland with him. Well I was going to be unemployed for six months now, so I agreed to go up.

I made a big mistake on the second part of my journey; I got on the coach at London and saw they had lots of leg room opposite the toilet at the back of the coach, so I sat opposite the toilet – big mistake. After hours of travelling all you could smell was the disinfectant swishing around in the toilet and it was making me feel quite ill.

When I arrived in the small village called Cree Town, my brother was waiting at the bus stop with a holdall. He took me over to where he was living, in a bed and breakfast. He introduced me to the landlord, and then said, "I'm leaving now, I will be living down the road."

I couldn't believe it. My brother spent all that time enticing me up there, and then he moves out as soon as I get there. Later that day I was sitting chatting with the landlord, when he said, "Your dad was down here a couple of weeks back and he said to me, 'Don't ask Steve why he looks different than his brother, it's because I'm not really his father.'"

I was fuming inside, when the landlord said that, because it was obvious my dad and brother had set me up, and got me up to Scotland for nothing but a sick joke. I wrote to Ann Marie the next day and asked her to find somewhere for me to live back in Tisbury, as I had been set up, it was all just a sick joke. Ann Marie found me a room after a few weeks, at the Bennet Arms in Tisbury, so after about seven weeks I got back on the coach back down to Tisbury.

It is now early December and I arrive back in Tisbury.

I didn't really want to stay in Tisbury; there was nothing there for me anymore, so I went into Salisbury and tracked down my friend, Jimmy. He used to live at Orchard House with me. He used to wake me up at about midnight when he got back from work, and he used to make us midnight feasts of salad cream sandwiches and a coffee. We would just sit there chatting and smoking for a couple of hours, then I'd go back to bed. Well I found Jimmy and asked if he would like to come on tour with the Switchback in March and in the meantime, would he help me find somewhere to live in Salisbury? He said yes to working on the Switchback and helped me find somewhere new to live while we waited to go on tour.

We found a bedsit in Castle Street – the landlord and landlady were very nice, they said I could move in while my housing benefits get sorted, so Jimmy helped me get my things from the Bennet Arms and I moved to Castle Street. I got hold of my Switchback boss and told him I had found someone to help us out for next year, and it was settled. Jimmy would come on tour with us.

I spent Christmas at my bedsit with my landlords; we went for a drink and had Christmas lunch together.

It's now January 1986 I'm 19, and I had a chat with my social worker about seeing my files after my dad said he wasn't my dad. So the social worker took me into the office one day, and went through the files, explaining he could only talk about my life, everything else was confidential. He went through how I ended up in children's homes. He said, "Your mum asked us to put you into care, so we put you in Starfield.

I said, "Hold on a minute, my mum has been telling me for years that it was my dad that put me in Starfield. Are you seriously telling me it was my mum?"

He said, "Yes, it was your mum."

I was disgusted with her. How could she lie, all these years?

He read on and said, "You asked to be put in a home so we put you in Orchard House." Everything else seemed to be in order, and there was no real way of finding out if my dad was lying to that landlord in Scotland.

One thing was clear in my mind after that chat with my social worker – my mum had lied for years and it was her that put me in Starfield, when I loved her with all my heart, and my dad was a sick paedophile who got away with giving me the belt for years.

*They're both sick and I don't want to be associated with them anymore. I'm going to change my surname by deed poll.*

A week or so later I found a solicitor and asked about changing my name. They explained the process and booked me an appointment in February to finalise the name change.

I had become good friends with the pub landlord at the Black Horse just down the road, and would look after the pub for him at lunchtimes, just for something to do. I didn't get paid, but I insisted he left the jukebox on constant play, so I had something to listen to. My favourite songs on his jukebox, were Nikita by Elton John, and Broken Wings by Mr Mister.

In the first week of February, I had a really odd week. First, Dawn found my bedsit and came and visited me, the next day, Sarah, who was one of the girls I lived at Orchard House with, and later had a quick fling with, also came and found me and we spent the day chatting. The next day I woke up really late, in a foul temper; it was about 10am, and I normally wake up at around 7am. The door bell rang, and I was in such a foul mood being woken up, I just wanted to throttle whoever was at the door for waking me. It was so out of character for me. Anyway, I went to answer the door feeling like telling whoever it was to get lost. I opened the door and I was gobsmacked – it was Ellen – she'd also found out where I lived. I invited her in.

I was all in a daze, she's the one person who I could not tell to go away. She was so different to all the other girls I'd been out with. So we spent the rest of the day chatting. I told Ellen I was just waiting to go back on tour. I also played this kind of weird song by Matt Bianco that always reminded me of her, it was just the instrumental side of the song and the way it played was what reminded me of Ellen. Anyway, Ellen left and we didn't arrange to meet up again or anything.

There was a day's break, then another stranger from the past had come to visit me; this time it was Stephanie, she was the sister of my old classmate that I used to visit in the weekends from Orchard House, the skinny girl I used to call fatty with a bit of affection. We got chatting and decided to go out with each other. We would kiss and I would fondle her breasts, but she seemed a bit of a tease, she wouldn't go any further than that.

It was now time to go and see the solicitor, to change my surname, but by this time I still hadn't thought of a name. I just couldn't think of something appropriate. Anyway I went to the solicitors; the solicitor got out the paperwork and said, "Ok, have you chosen a name?" and Grey shot out my mouth. He said, "Are you sure about that?" and I thought for a few seconds. *Well this is about good and bad, black and white, yin and yang. Yes, Grey is perfect.* So I said yes, Grey with an e, and the deed was done. I always approach life weighing up good and bad, black and white, so the surname Grey is very apt.

Stephanie called round one evening, but I had to pop down the pub, as I was in the pool team, so I kept having a match, then popping back to Stephanie. She was being a bit annoying that night; she kept on about a DJ friend, and I got the impression she fancied the guy. I took her to the bottom of her street – it was about 11pm. She wanted me to leave her there and she would go home alone, so we said goodbye, and Stephanie made her way up the road, and I stayed until I saw her get home safely, but instead of going into her house, she started talking to someone in a van. My thought was, *It's that bloody DJ, she's talking to that DJ.*

I got a Valentine's Day card from Stephanie a couple of days later. I was still angry with her and tore up the card and threw it in the bin. Later that day I spotted Stephanie, parked up the road from where I live, so I went back to the house, got the card out of the bin, and then went back to the car and tapped on her window on the passenger's side. She wound the window down with a big smile, and I threw the torn up card on her lap and left her to her stupid games. I assumed the driver was probably the DJ she kept going on about.

It was now March '86, time to get hold of Jimmy and take a bus over to Stainers Yard, to get ready for our summer tour with the Switchback.

This time we started the tour at Southampton Common; there were a couple of things I remember about this place. Firstly I was woken up at about 7am by the noise of a hot air balloon being blown up, not far from the rides, and there was a wrestling ring set up right next to our ride. I got to see a wrestling match between one of my favourite wrestlers, Iron Fist Clive Myers, versus a wrestler everyone loved to hate, Mark Rollerball Rocco. As I was a big wrestling fan, I stood on the hill of the Switchback and watched the match – they were two very big wrestling celebrities of that time.

Next we went to a place called Clarendon House, just outside Salisbury. This time we were on a film set in old clothes from about the 1930s for a film called

A Day After the Fair. I recall Tony, who was a big strong man who drove one of the loads, called us all over and said, "Watch this," and he grabbed the front of this Massey Ferguson Tractor, gave a couple of grunts, and tipped up the front of the tractor, then put it down and laughed his head off. He said I was driving along in the tractor, and with the weight of the water butt on the back it was slightly heavier than the front of the tractor, so the steering was really light. I thought I'd see if I could lift the front and it was dead easy. He then said, "You wait. When the camera men come I'll do it again and wind the buggers up." They were gobsmacked when they saw how strong Tony was.

Then we drove all the way up to London, to do filming with Wilson's Fair, for a celebrity It's a Knockout show, to be televised. Two of the celebrities there were Geoff Capes, who used to be the World's Strongest Man, and Samantha Fox, a page three girl for the Sun newspaper. I can't remember the rest of the celebrities' names, as only these two came on the ride and had a chat with us. While we were with Wilson's Fair, we took a tea break, and watched the Wilson's crews putting up their rides. Their rides went up incredibly quick; they would just push a button, and everything would just unfold from the centre truck, even the dodgems opened out like a concertina and were built within half an hour.

Next we joined an old fairground company called Carters, who travelled with old rides only, so we blended in nicely with them. We went to a couple of steam rallies, then back to Southampton Common.

This time I met a girl and started messing about with her; her friend was interested in another work mate called Harry. The girl that was interested in Harry told me I bruised her friend's arm earlier, and that we have to be careful, because Jayne has a rare blood disease, and she has to be careful, as a knock could cause her blood to clot. We had a nice week, with these girls coming to chat with us, and on the final night, we would have gone all the way, but it was the time of the month, but we did still have a good night in bed. We moved on the next day to Wooky Hole in Somerset – that was a quiet week. I missed Jayne. I felt sorry for her too having such a rare blood disorder.

Next we moved on to Iron Bridge Gauge in the Midlands. This was an old-time museum, where all the staff dressed in old-time clothes, and made things the old-fashioned ways.

We went to a couple more fairs and steam rallies on our way back down to Wiltshire. One time a lorry was flashing at us from behind, so we pulled over, and the driver told us a wheel had come off our back trailer. He was right, it had shot across the dual carriageway 200 yards down the road; we were lucky not to have lost the organ that the wheel came off of.

We finished the tour back at Stourpaine, and the boss could not afford to keep us on through the winter, so Jimmy and everyone else went back home and I contacted my sister in Wolverhampton and decided to go and live with her.

So in August 1986 I moved to Wolverhampton.

# Chapter 4

## *My life between the Switchback and getting married*

When I first moved in with my sister, we had years to catch up on. We talked a lot about the abuse we had been through, and how badly our mum and dad had treated us over the years. It was then that I learned, my sister had actually given the police the belts that my dad had used on me, and she had told the police all about my abuse when she told them about her own sexual abuse from my father. I told her that the children's home boss told me he would not let the police talk to me at that time, because I was not living with her, so the police never got to see the scars on my back, otherwise he would have got the sentence he deserved. My sister went on to say the sexual abuse had been going on since she was 4 years old, way back as far as she could remember. I thought it was awful that my dad should only get a two-year prison sentence for this.

My sister and I got really close after finding out about each other's lives apart. Wolverhampton wasn't too bad; the cost of living was much cheaper than

Salisbury, there was so much to do and so many different cultures all in one place.

We were both unemployed at Christmas and both our giros were delayed in the post, so on Christmas Day, all we had to eat for our dinner was plain brown spaghetti on toast, but our giros came between Christmas and my birthday New Year's day, so we made up for it on my birthday and had a nice meal and some drink.

So it's now 1987 and I am 20 years old.

In January, I was thinking about Ellen and her faith in Buddhism and decided to get some books from the library and read about it. What I like most about Buddhism, is that it teaches you to be non-materialistic, and in some ways there were Christian values too, so I decided I would like to become a Christian Buddhist, which exists as a mixture of both faiths.

I wrote to Ellen and told her I had been studying Buddhism, and how much I liked a lot of what Buddhism stands for, and my faith had moved more towards Buddhism.

A week later, I received a letter from Ellen, saying after listening to that song by Matt Bianco in my bedsit, she thought I was Christian listening to the lyrics, so Ellen went away to learn Christianity and joined the Mormons. I thought, *Oh no, that wasn't supposed to happen.* I didn't even know the lyrics of the song, and it was just the tune that used to remind me of her, not the lyrics. Now we have both gone in opposite directions to learn more about each other – that definitely was not supposed to happen.

I told my sister, "I want to buy Ellen a special ring,

to show how much I care for her," so we went into town, and we came across this pretty ring that was made up of different coloured stones. On further enquiries in the jewellers, the ring was an eternity ring, whose stones actually spelled out the word D.E.A.R.E.S.T. The stones were Diamond, Emerald, Amethyst, Ruby, Emerald, Sapphire and Topaz. I thought the ring was absolutely perfect and bought it on the spot.

The next day I caught a train down to Salisbury, went to Ellen's house, and gave her the ring. I was very shy about what the ring meant, and I said to Ellen, "The stones spell out something, but you will need to go to a jewellers to find out what it spells." I was just too shy to come straight out with it. After a couple of hours with Ellen, I caught a train back to Wolverhampton. I did learn one thing from all of this, and that was to listen to lyrics of songs where I like the tunes, before telling someone it reminds me of them.

In February I put my name down on the Council waiting list for a house or flat in Wolverhampton. Also my sister told me she was pregnant and due in September, so it was a good thing to get on the housing list, so my sister could have the bedroom ready for her baby when it arrived.

Around April '87, I was fed up of being unemployed, and just wanted to get away for a few days, so I thought, *I will nip down to my younger brother in Salisbury and spend a few days with him*, only I didn't tell my sister where I was going, I just got up and caught the train to Salisbury, a spur of the moment type of thing.

After getting to my younger brother's flat a couple of hours later, I thought, *I best phone my sister and let her know where I am.*

My sister said, "Why, did you just go off like that? I was worried about you. I even phoned Mum to see if you had gone to her."

I explained I just needed a break, and I that I would phone her back again in a couple of days, just to see how things were going, and we left it at that.

Two days later, which was now Wednesday, I phoned my sister again, and she was all in a panic and upset. She said to me, "You have to get out of there and come home, Dad is after you, Mum sent him after you."

I said, "What do you mean?"

My sister explained, all she did was phone Mum to say that she had heard from me and I was safe and well, staying with our younger brother, and my mum told my sister she was going to send our dad after me, to sort me out. I told my sister not to worry. "I am not going to come home yet though, I wanted a week's holiday and I'm going to have it. I'm not running from Dad, I'm not scared of him. He can come and get me if he wants, I will be waiting for him."

On Friday afternoon I was looking out my brother's flat window, overlooking Elizabeth Gardens, when sure enough my dad turned up in a car. I saw him get out of the car and he let an Alsatian out the back of the car. He looked up to the flat and our eyes met. I was just built up with anger, that he had the nerve to think he was going to come and sort me out. If looks could kill, between the way my dad and I looked at each other, anyone standing between us would be dead – it was pure hate from both sides.

I was ready for a fight, but to my disbelief my dad did not cross the road and come to the flat, instead he took his dog into Elizabeth Gardens. My immediate thought was, *You bastard, you did that to give me the chance to run away, and I am not running anywhere.* I was absolutely fuming. I said to my younger brother, "If he thinks I'm going to run he's got another thing coming," and with that I quickly and angrily ran down the stairs, and walked straight over to my dad in the park. My first words were, "Why did you tell that Landlord in Scotland you're not my father?" and he just gave me a sick grin.

With that, my younger brother turned up, and cooled the situation and said, "Let's go for a drink." So we all went to a pub in town. My brother and dad talked a lot, I had nothing to say. A couple of pints later we left the pub, and were back outside my brother's flat, when my dad turned to me and said, "Why are you down here causing trouble? Why are you always running away and causing trouble?"

I, without thinking, just said, "Mum is the one causing trouble. I'm here for a week's holiday, she's the one who's stirring it up by calling you."

To my surprise he just shook my hand and said, "Take care of yourself," then he started talking to my brother, then he left. I could not believe what just happened.

The next day I went back to my sister in Wolverhampton.

At the end of May I had got fed up with being

unemployed, so I thought I would go and do some voluntary work somewhere.

About half a mile away on another estate, there was a Y.W.C.A. Young Woman's Christian Association, in a flat at the back of a large housing estate, so I popped in there and looked around the wall posters to see what they did, then spoke to a couple of staff there, including the manager. They had projects like a toy library, a crèche, and latch key project, where kids can go to the Y.W.C.A. straight after school if their parents weren't home. They told me they run schemes for the community to use or they help run, by becoming volunteers.

I said, "Do you have a brochure to go door to door and tell people about your projects? Because I think that's what you need."

We talked a little more, and I said I would like to become a volunteer. When I got up to leave after we finished chatting, the manager said, "How would you like a job here on a community programme? We have a job vacancy available on a community programme if you're interested."

So I accepted and set about making a brochure and finding out about all the services the Y.W.C.A provide, then I went door to door on the estate telling people all about the Y.W.C.A and how it was looking to expand existing projects, create new projects, and recruit volunteers to help run these projects. It was an exciting job with positive results, more local people were coming in to use the centre, or help run it.

There was a woman called Glenda, who started working on a community programme with the

Y.W.C.A, a week after I started. Glenda was a very troubled woman in her late forties, who was going through a very messy divorce and talked a lot about it to other staff, and broke down crying a lot. Glenda only lived round the corner from me, so she offered to give me a lift to work in the mornings.

There was a girl who used to live opposite us, the back of the houses would be facing each other and my bedroom faced opposite this girl's bedroom. This girl would wave to me, whenever I went to my bedroom window. One day we met in the street, and she came back to my sister's flat with me. Her name was Julia. She was a nice girl but a bit too young for me. Julia was still a schoolgirl. She came round a few times, and I said to my sister, "What shall I do? She's a nice girl, but too young to go out with."

My sister just said, "Let her down gently, tell her you can't go out with each other because of the age gap."

So I let Julia down as nicely as possible. She went home and a couple of days later she handed me a tape and said, "There's a song on there for you." The song was called Almaz by Randy Crawford. I did not really understand the lyrics, though, and Julia stayed away after that.

In July '87 I was offered a council flat in Heath town, Wolverhampton. When I went to look at the flat, I couldn't believe I had been offered a ground floor flat, when you could see elderly people about six floors up, looking out of their windows on the opposite side of the road. I also noticed the woodwork had dents in it around the lock area of the door frame, where someone had tried to break in. So when I moved in, I bought these badly fitting net curtains, so that I would look poor, and no one would bother breaking in.

About a week after I moved in this sweet old lady knocked on my door and said, "I'm your neighbour, I thought you may like these," and passed me some nearly new net curtains. I said thank you, and when she left, I thought, *Oh my god, I didn't mean it to look so bad that the old lady felt sorry for me and gave me some net curtains,* so I thought, *I'd better put them up if it looks that bad and I don't want to offend the sweet old lady by not changing them.*

In August I was having a good wander around the flats, and discovered some brilliant graffiti on some of the walls and on the staircases; the work was by a chap called Goldie – his art work was amazing. I took photos of his work. Unfortunately I lost the photos years later during moving, but Goldie had painted this big picture, that looked space aged, and it was as if he had caught Heath Town in a bubble, but somewhere in the future like a space age picture. It was amazing. Also, in the shopping precinct part of the flats was a walkway, and Goldie had painted Weetabix characters doing all sorts of Olympic sports, it was very clever and certainly brightened the place up.

In the second week of September my sister had a little girl.

Also in September, Glenda from the Y.W.C.A and I were sent on a college course, to go every Friday. As the college was in town, and my flat was closest to town, I would invite Glenda back to my flat for lunch. Unfortunately by the third week of going back to my flat Glenda revealed to me that she was fantasising about me the night before. I did not know what to say at the time because she was really serious, and she was old enough to be my mother. She took me totally by surprise, so I suggested it was time to go back to college, and we went back to college. I was in total disbelief about what Glenda had just told me. When I got home from college I thought the situation through a bit more, and thought, *Well I didn't lead Glenda on, but with her divorce being a messy one, perhaps she was just getting a bit confused.* Nevertheless, it was going to make working together very awkward, so the next day I went in to my boss and explained what had happened in our lunch break, and the manager of the Y.W.C.A said, "Well, Glenda will have to leave, because another member of staff is leaving in a couple of weeks and I want you to take over their job."

I felt awful about the boss's decision because Glenda was such a messed up woman, and much needed the support of the staff at the Y.W.C.A. The deputy manager was outside round the corner and I bumped into her, she could see I was looking upset, so I explained to her what had happened and that I was concerned for Glenda. If she lost her job she would be devastated and she needed the support of the staff, so the deputy said I could go to the community programme office and they would give me a different job, and the deputy said she would phone them and explain the situation. "That way there will be no need for the manager to get rid of Glenda and you'll have a safe job as well." So that's what we did.

The next day I went to the community programme

office, and they offered me a job closer to my home, to work in a community maintenance team in a project called the Steel House Lane Project.

There were only three team members before I came along, but after I met the team, I felt the job was perfect for me. The boss was Polish, and there was an Indian lad, another lad from Wolverhampton, and myself, and we all got on brilliantly straight from the start.

Our job was to keep the streets clean in the community and do a bit of painting and decorating, gardening, repair windows, all kinds of DIY jobs in a run-down community. I loved the job, except for one thing, it could be thirsty work and people would offer you a cup of tea, but the tea was most often foul, because most of the people we worked for used sterilised milk in their tea and it was disgusting.

I spent Christmas Day and my birthday with my sister, her daughter, and her boyfriend.

It is now 1988 and I am 21 years old.

In January my younger sister who had been brought up by my mum, fell out with my mum and asked if she could come and stay with me, so I said yes.

My younger sister came to live with me for about three weeks, and in that time she exchanged letters back and forth with my mum. They made up and my younger sister moved back with my mum in Devon. I don't think my sister was comfortable living in flats right next to a big city after being brought up in little villages; it was all a bit overwhelming for her. My younger sister and I had become much closer for her stay with me, and we stayed in touch after that.

We're now in May and my contract with the community programme is going to end in June. My younger sister had moved into a flat with her boyfriend, so I asked her if I could come and stay with them until I get a job and get a flat myself and she said yes, so when the community programme ended I gave the keys to my flat back to the Council and moved to Kingsbridge, Devon.

It's June 1988. I'm 21 and I'm off for yet another fresh start. I caught the train and bus down to my sister in Kingsbridge, Devon. On my first day in Kingsbridge, I went for an interview at Gateways Supermarket. My sister and her boyfriend were already working there. Gateways told my sister the next day, I had got a job at Gateways, immediate start if I liked, so I took the job.

We were living in a place called Kildare Apartments, and my sister's flat was a little cramped with me sleeping in the lounge. There was this chap called Trevor who was in charge of looking after the tenants and taking rents and so on, on behalf of the landlord. I had a word with Trevor to see if he could get me a flat of my own. Trevor was a nice old chap, he loved people dropping in to say hello. Anyway, around mid-July, Trevor told me I could rent a flat in Kildare Mews, which was at the back of Kildare Apartments, and I moved into the flat.

At work, I worked on the greengrocery department all the time, so I made it my business to learn how to run the department properly. I also took an equal interest in the wines and spirits department, because it was in the same aisle as the greengrocery department, so it was worth learning both with the view to becoming a department manager in either section.

In August the wines and spirits department manager quit his job, so I went straight to the store manager and applied for the job of wines and spirits manager. The store manager said yes, I could have the job.

The greengrocery department manager went to the store manager and told him if I become wines and spirits manager, she will quit her job as greengrocery department manager, as she can't run it without me.

The store manager called me back to the office and explained the new situation and said, "So now the greengrocery department manager has quit I would like you to become greengrocery department manager, as you are the best person for that job." So I accepted the greengrocery department manager's job instead of wines and spirits. This job came with a condition, the pay was set at £105 a week and I couldn't earn any overtime, and the job takes as long as it takes to do it properly.

In September I started going out with one of the staff called Mary; before I knew what was happening Mary had moved in with me. I had taken Mary round to see my mum once, they seemed to get on ok. After about four weeks together, Mary wanted to get engaged, and I put the brakes on. I said I was not completely over Ellen yet, I wasn't ready for that sort of commitment, and deep down I still wanted to be with Ellen. Mary wanted to talk about it some more but I didn't, so we left it at that.

Around the same time, that Mary asked me to get engaged. Trevor told us that the people that own the flat we were renting wanted to sell the flat.

A week after Trevor told us about the flat going up for sale and Mary asking to get engaged, one of the girls at work came up and told me, "Mary is up in the staff room showing everyone a letter from your ex, Ellen. Ellen has told Mary that she is a lesbian, so if Mary wants to marry you, go ahead." I was furious. It meant that Mary had gone through my address book and wrote to Ellen behind my back. So, I made up my mind. *When I get home I will be packing Mary's bags, and chucking her stuff out of my flat.*

I went and told Trevor I had kicked Mary out, and why, and Trevor said, "It's just as well, because Mary was trying to buy the flat for you both, she'd already seen me on her own about buying it." So I had a lucky escape I guess.

I must mention, I used to have two staff that used to come and assist me a lot. One girl I called Smiler, because she was always in a bad mood and I loved to wind her up and make her smile. There was another girl I would call Trouble, because she was a very hard worker but had a good sense of humour too, and when she did not work with me, she would work with someone else that I would call Double Trouble, because when they were together, they were fun to joke around with. I also got on well with a chap called Mike, who used to take in all the deliveries. Our little group worked closely together and kept each other happy on the days when things were a bit hectic and stressful – we looked out for each other.

I went over to my mum for Christmas, but I spent my birthday alone, so we are now into January 1989 and I'm 22 years old.

In February I went one evening to view one of

two flats that had become available in Kildare Apartments; while I was viewing a flat there was also an attractive girl, introduced to me as Sarah, who had come to view the other flat.

We both moved into the flats in the next couple of days. Sarah came and knocked on my door a couple of nights after moving in, we got chatting and ended up making love on the floor, then a while after Sarah went back to her flat. A couple of days later I went to see Sarah, and we talked and she explained she could not go out with me as she was already engaged to a man, so I left her alone.

About five weeks later Sarah moved out and went back home, without saying goodbye or anything, she just left.

One day I started thinking about Ann Marie. I wondered if she had forgiven me yet for what I had done to her. I wanted to visit her and bury any bad feelings Ann Marie still had towards me, so on my next day off work, I went down to Bournemouth to visit Ann Marie. When I got there I found that Ann Marie had moved on. Fortunately I was given the right address to go to, and when I got to the right address, it was flats, with a security buzzer, where you have to ring the bell of the flat you want, then the flat owner presses a button to release the communal door. I wasn't sure if Ann Marie would press the buzzer to let me in, so after I pressed the doorbell I kept quiet, and while Ann Marie said, "Who is it?" she also pressed the door release, so I shot in quickly and started walking up the stairs.

Ann Marie stood at the top of the stairs and when she saw me, she shrieked, "It's Steve!" in a happy, excited way, then she disappeared. By time I reached the flat, Ann Marie and her boyfriend were standing at the door, and they invited me in for a cup of coffee.

Ann Marie got some photo albums out and told me how all her family were doing, and at one point, Ann Marie surprised me. She went over to her fireplace and picked up a photo of her and her boyfriend, then she went over to the skylight and faced me, looking at the photo it was as if she was comparing me against her boyfriend. Then she went back to the fireplace and slammed the photo down, as if she was disappointed. I had to leave shortly after to go and get a room to stay in for the night and something to eat, but they said I could come back after I was sorted.

When I went back to the flat later, Ann Marie was having a bath and I was left talking to the boyfriend, who didn't seem too keen to have me there. About three quarters of an hour had passed and I got the distinct impression Ann Marie was not going to come out the bathroom for whatever reason, so I made my excuses and left. When I shouted goodbye to Ann Marie through the bathroom door, she replied goodbye, but it sounded like she was crying, and really upset. I didn't know if they had had a big row with me turning up out of the blue or what, but I felt I had at least been forgiven by Ann Marie's initial response to seeing me on the stairs. So I went to my room I booked for the night, and thought, *Well Ann Marie is with someone, so she must be happy, and at least she spoke to me, that's the best I could hope for in the circumstances*, and the next day I went home.

In April I learned that students at work were earning overtime pay, and earning more than me as general assistants. I thought it was ridiculous so I looked for a job with higher pay, and later that month, I handed in my notice and went to work for Jades Components, an electrical components factory; they offered me the job of dispatch supervisor, on a basic wage of about £116 a week, plus overtime available, so I used to work Saturday mornings as well for the overtime.

My job at Jades was to work at the end of the line, counting goods for dispatch, putting the correct paperwork with the goods, packing the goods in boxes, and attaching the correct labels on the boxes to ship them off all over the world. I would then put them on the correct dispatch vehicles. When it was quiet in the dispatch area, I would go down and help this lad called Chris with varnish dipping – dipping electrical components into varnish – we used to get as high as a kite doing that job.

By the end of July, I was beginning to get bored of the job, doing the same job over and over. I was beginning to regret leaving Gateways, so, I wrote to Gateways to see if there was any chance I could go back to work for them. At the time the store had a new manager, and a couple of weeks went by and the store manager did not reply, so I went over his head and wrote to head office. Within a week I received a phone call from the new store manager, he said, "I have been told by head office to call you in for an interview."

When I went to the interview, the new manager said, "I have to give you your old job back, on a month's trial. If you do well, you will get a pay rise to £116 a week, but if you don't do well you will be out." I said ok, and went back to Gateways.

After a month back at Gateways, I knew I had done well that month, taking over £1,000, more a week than the previous department manager, so when the area manager came round, I asked the store manager to ask the area manager to approve my pay rise. The store manager said he would, but made excuses later for not asking, saying he was too busy. The next week, the same thing happened again. The area manager came and the store manager made his excuses. The day after this happened for the second time, I thought, *I'm not taking this crap anymore, he either pays what he offered or I'm quitting*. So that morning I went straight to the manager's office and I said to the manager, "I want you to phone head office and get this pay rise authorised or I am walking out this store."

He said, "Go to the staff room and I will call you back, once I have spoken to head office."

The manager called me back and told me head office would not approve the rise, so I said, "Ok, stick your job," and left.

I went back to Trevor who acts on behalf of our landlord, and I explained the situation, Trevor in turn spoke to my landlord.

My landlord said to Trevor his wife is about to open a small shop in Chesterfield, would I like to come and stay with them in Chesterfield and help out in the shop? So I said yes, and my landlord arranged to come and pick me up in a couple of weeks.

One day I was in town, and I overheard these two

ladies talking about the Sarah I had made love with back in February. One lady was saying to the other, Sarah's fiancée had left her, because she was pregnant and he knew the baby was not his.

I had not seen Sarah since March, so I wrote her a letter saying, 'I just found out you are pregnant, and I'm moving to Chesterfield, in a week. Will you please tell me if I am the father of your baby?' Then I hand delivered the letter to Sarah's house.

Later that day Sarah came to see me and told me I was not the father. I was not entirely convinced Sarah was telling the truth, but I couldn't prove otherwise, so I had to take her word for it. We chatted for a while, then Sarah left, and I was left in doubt as to whether Sarah had told me the truth, but I guess I would never know now.

The next week my landlord came and picked me up and I went to live with his family in Chesterfield.

When I was living with my landlord's family, they were nice to me and treated me like part of the family. I helped out in the sandwich shop they owned for my keep, but finding a permanent job was proving very difficult, so I stayed in contact with my older sister in Wolverhampton, keeping in mind if I could not find permanent work in Chesterfield by Christmas, I would stay with my sister for a while.

Christmas came and there was no permanent job on the horizon, so I said goodbye to the family and moved over to my sister in Wolverhampton.

I got a surprise letter forwarded to me from Chesterfield. It was a letter out of the blue, from Sarah, the girl who said I wasn't the father of her baby. Out of the blue Sarah sent me a letter, telling me she had had a baby boy that she had named Mark Stephen, the birthdate of December, and his birth weight. I don't know why Sarah sent me the letter out of the blue with so much detail, after all, last time we spoke she said the baby was not mine, so it did not make sense that Sarah wrote to me out of the blue. I thought I would never hear from her again, to be honest. Anyway I sent Sarah a congratulations card, but never heard from her again. I did wonder if the baby was mine, still, and I was surprised the baby had my first name as its second name.

On my birthday, January 1st 1990, I was 23 years old, and I thought about my situation, living with my sister who had her own family, and how difficult it was to get a job before, so after my birthday I contacted my mum and asked if I could stay with her for a short while in Kingsbridge, so I could get a job and a flat. My mum agreed, so mid-January I moved back down to Kingsbridge.

About the third week in January, I looked through the jobs section of the local Gazette and applied for a care assistant job at South Efford House in Aveton Gifford, which was a retirement home for the elderly. I was invited for an interview by the home owner/manager. As I had not had any experience in care work and the fact that most of the residents were female, the manager said, "I can't really give you a job as a care assistant, but as you have experience in maintenance work, would you like to come and be a live-in maintenance person, working sixteen hours a week to pay for your keep? That was perfect for me, so I accepted the job, and moved in at the beginning of February.

In March when I visited my mum, I told her, "I am looking for extra part-time work, as I am only working sixteen hours a week."

My mum said she'd ask the thatcher who was thatching their roof if he needed an assistant or knew of anyone else who did. The thatcher gave my mum the number for a thatcher called Alan, who was looking for an apprentice full-time, so I called Alan and he offered me a job. It was lucky I had bought myself a motorbike by then. It was only a 125cc Honda, but that's as big a bike as I was able to ride, as I had not passed my test.

It was not long after moving into South Efford House that I found out that it is haunted. About the same time as I started my thatching job, one night the home manager, the assistant manager and I were all sleeping on the second floor of this three-storey house that was built in 1770. We kept getting woken up by this banging noise coming from somewhere within the building. After about the third time of hearing this banging, we all decided to go and split up in the home. The manager went to check out the first floor, the assistant manager checked out the ground floor, and I went outside the building to see if I could pinpoint the sound. We all met up after about ten minutes on the top floor. The banging continued but none of us could find the cause. While we are on the subject of South Efford House being haunted, I will mention a couple of other things now, as I may forget later.

One day three residents in separate rooms, all overlooking a big tree on the front lawn, all said they could see a couple in tracksuits sitting by the tree.

That was really strange, because these three residents had not come in contact with each other that day, and they weren't the type to make up stories – they were all serious, and this couple in a tracksuit, had also been spotted by other residents in later days. I thought it was strange that they would all see a couple in a tracksuit by the tree, because tracksuits are not really that old, so how did these people appear by the tree in tracksuits? But the residents were genuine enough in what they could see.

The other thing that most night staff experienced, is that when you're in the lounge at night, you can hear fast footsteps going along the hall above the lounge. They're too fast for a resident, and when you go and check on the residents, they're all sound asleep.

There is a story that years ago a ferryman hung himself on the staircase in the home, so it is probably him causing all the banging and footsteps in the hallway, but I haven't a clue about the couple in the tracksuits.

I was enjoying my thatching job. Alan and his other employee, Stephen, were really nice to work with, and I was enjoying learning new skills.

There was a new member of staff at South Efford House; she was a good ten years older than me, but very attractive for her age. She was married and had two sons. I fancied her quite a lot; within two months we would sneak up and pinch each other's bottom, many times, but neither of us took it any further.

In May I had an accident on my motorbike and came off and damaged the bike. I had a chat with my thatching boss and he gave me £250 wear and tear for me using my bike for work, and lent me the rest of the money to buy myself another motorbike. So I bought a second-hand CB 125 Twin, it was a nice heavy bike and handled well in the rain.

At Christmas I rode up to my sister in Wolverhampton, and rode back just after my birthday, so we are now in January 1991 and I'm 24 years old.

It was snowing on my way home, and it was freezing. I had to keep stopping outside phone boxes, then going in the boxes to have a cigarette and warm up a bit. I even accidentally ended up on the motorway with my L plates on.

I'm still enjoying thatching, although it can be a bit scary out on the bike on some of the icy back lanes.

I'm still living at South Efford House and enjoying doing maintenance work.

Around June, there was a member of staff called Donna, who was married, with a young daughter, about 2 years old. Donna usually only worked weekends, but she was asked to do a night shift. As I lived in at the home, I went down and had a chat with Donna; she had a snack box, and I jokingly asked if she had bought enough for me as well, and Donna had bought two of everything, so we sat and talked and ate. We talked so much that we fell for each other and Donna wanted to leave her husband. Donna said she would ask Angela, the home owner, if she could come and live on the top floor. Angela agreed, unaware of the night Donna and I had just had. Angela went on holiday for a couple of weeks. Donna and I enjoyed making love either in my bedroom, or in a barn just up the road, behind the home.

When Angela came back, the deputy manager said to me, "I know you're having an affair with Donna; I'm going to have to report it to Angela." When Angela found out, she told Donna she didn't want to become involved in an affair, so Donna must go back home. Donna and I were gutted, but there was nothing we could do about it, as I lived in the home, so Donna arranged to go back home.

The next weekend Donna worked we found it hard to stay apart and agreed to meet up on Bantham Beach, after work. When we met we both struggled to find a way forward, because South Efford was my home and part-time job, so Donna said in the end, "We have to end the relationship."

We continued to work together for about another three weekends, and I was finding it hard to cope, with Donna keep coming back into my life in the weekends as if nothing had happened. I asked Donna to quit her weekend job at South Efford and go and find a job elsewhere, or I would leave, but as this was my home I would prefer it if she left. Donna just said she wasn't going anywhere.

I contacted one of the staff who used to work in Orchard House Children's Home, and asked if he could put me up for a while; his name was Tim and he lived in Wilton, near Salisbury. Tim said I could stay at his house for a while.

I had a word with my thatching boss, and explained that I needed to get out of South Efford House as soon as possible, and I had somewhere to stay near Salisbury. I asked Alan, while I move to Salisbury for now, could he find affordable accommodation in the South Brent area, to live nearer to him and make it easier to get to work? So Alan agreed to look out for somewhere for me.

I left South Efford House and went down to Tim in Wilton.

On the first day in Wilton I needed to use the toilets in the town car park. While I was there, I saw my ex, Stephanie, chatting to a guy; she was looking at me then started laughing and ran off with this guy through the town. I was annoyed. I thought she was making fun of me, so when I got back to Tim's I wrote her a letter and told her she was childish, laughing at me and running off, she needs to grow up, and I sent it to her old address.

I visited Ellen, my ex-girlfriend, who was living in Salisbury. Ellen introduced me to her son, who was about 5 years old. I didn't think Ellen was a lesbian as she had written to my girlfriend in 1988. I think my girlfriend must have written something that really upset her. It was nice to see Ellen again, and her mum. Ellen had passed her driving test and took her son and me for a drive; when we got back to Ellen's house, I left, thinking, *Well Ellen must have a boyfriend somewhere if she has a son now, and she seems very happy with her life.* So I just said goodbye and that was the last time we saw each other.

I stayed in touch with Alan, my thatching boss, and in September he found me a caravan to rent on a holiday park in Ashburton, called Waterleat Caravan Park; the rent was only £30 a week and it was a lovely location. The caravan had a lounge, kitchen, double bedroom and a shower, and it was set back, at the back of the caravan park next to a stream, and the lounge window had a view overlooking the caravan park and the woods beyond. Ashburton was a lovely friendly small town, whose main political party was the Monster Raving Loony Party, led by Screaming Lord Sutch.

I visited South Efford House shortly after moving into my caravan, only to learn that Donna, who I had the affair with, quit her job the week after I left South Efford House, so when I went back to my caravan I wrote an angry letter to Donna, saying how annoyed I was that she would not leave when I asked her to, but as soon as I left, she quit her job anyway and made me homeless when it wasn't necessary. I wrote her this angry letter, but she never replied.

One day I was in the West Alvington area of Kingsbridge, and I bumped into Sarah, the girl who said I wasn't the father of her son, but had contacted me out of the blue to tell me she had had a son, and told me in the letter his name and birth weight. Sarah was walking with her mum and had the baby in a push chair. Sarah had a look of horror on her face when I started to walk towards her, as if I was going to take the baby or something like that, when all I wanted to do was say hello. We had a little chat, then I left and went back to my caravan.

When I got back to my caravan I started to think, *Why did Sarah contact me out of the blue and tell me her son's birth weight, and why did she give her son my first name as his middle name, and why did she react as if I was going to take her baby? Perhaps it's because the baby was really mine after all. How will I get Sarah to tell the truth?* I thought, *Well Sarah may have a boyfriend and be happy now, but if Mark Stephen is my son, I have a right to know, and besides, I would want to offer money each week to help provide for Mark*

*Stephen, if he is my son.* So I wrote a letter asking Sarah if she would have a DNA test, so I could know for sure if the baby is mine or not, and so that I can provide for him if I am the father.

A couple of weeks later I received a letter from a Kingsbridge doctor, telling me to leave Sarah alone and that she does not need a DNA test. I thought, *Well there is nothing else I can do now, but I'm not convinced she is telling the truth, and the doctor knows nothing, because her long-term fiancée could not get her pregnant and he left her knowing it was someone else that did get Sarah pregnant –* that's why I still believe Sarah was lying. So I thought, *Ok, there is nothing else I can do now to get Sarah to tell the truth, but if I ever get someone called Mark Stephen tap me on the shoulder and tell me I am their dad, I will tell them I did try to find out the truth, and tell them the doctor's name who refused to do the DNA test. That's all I can do.*

At Christmas, I spent Christmas Day with my mum. Then it was my birthday on January 1$^{st}$ 1992, and I am now aged 25 years old.

In mid-January '92, I got new neighbours. A small towing caravan was parked up in front of my caravan, and a couple about the same age as me were living in it.

My motorbike engine was on its way out, so I had a chat with Alan, and he gave me £250 wear and tear on my bike and lent me £250, and I got £350 part-exchange on my bike and bought a newer Honda 125 NSF. It was a faster bike with a power band – it could do 96 miles per hour, overtaking on the A38, so there was need to pass my test when the legal limit was 70mph anyway.

In February/March time, I walked near the

caravan next to me and the girl who lived there with her husband started talking to me. Her name was Susan. We got talking and she told me her husband had gone away for the week, I told Susan she was welcome over to mine for a coffee, whenever she liked. Later that day, Susan came over. We watched a film together, getting closer and closer as the film went on, until we ended up making love, and we carried on making love for the next four days, whenever we got the chance.

Susan made up her mind she wanted to leave her husband and live with me, but not in England; she wanted me to move to Ontario with her. I did not have a passport so I could not leave there and then, but we went into Newton Abbott, the nearest big town, and applied for a passport for me. Then Susan said she wanted me to go to London Airport with her and see her off, and she went back to Ontario alone, but gave me a contact phone number I could keep in touch with her on, until my passport arrived.

I told Alan, my thatching boss, that I had got in a bit of a sticky patch with Susan, as he was a good listener, almost like a father figure.

I stayed in contact by phone with Susan for about three weeks, when her friend answered the phone instead of her, and her friend said Susan's husband came and collected her, and she didn't know where they had gone. So that was the end of that. There was nothing I could do, although in December '92 I did have a telegram forwarded to me from the caravan park – it was from Susan from Ontario. It was a short message to say, 'This is Susan. Please contact me on this number.'

Well I tried the number, but it was missing an area code, so I never got through or found out what Susan wanted.

In July I visited Angela at South Efford House, and she persuaded me to work there on Sundays in the kitchen.

In August the recession was affecting the thatching business and we were running out of work. At the same time Angela asked me one Sunday if I would come back and live there and do full-time work, both in maintenance and in the kitchen. So, I said yes I would.

I gave Alan two weeks' notice and told him, "As work is running out, it is for the best if I go back to South Efford House." Then he and Stephen may just survive the recession, well that's what I hoped anyway.

In September I moved back to South Efford House and started full-time work there, either running the kitchen in the afternoons and evenings, or doing maintenance work. One day I went to the village shop, and I saw this girl dressed in overalls covered from head to toe in cow muck. I remember thinking, *That girl still looks pretty, even covered in muck. I bet she's a nice girl who doesn't go to clubs and dance around her handbag.*

# Chapter 5

## *Marriage, work life, children, and voluntary roles*

In October a new girl started work at South Efford House. Her name was Louisa. It wasn't long before I discovered she was the same girl I'd seen covered in cow muck at the shop. From then on, I really wanted to go out with her; she was different than your average girl. I didn't want someone that does pubs and clubs, I liked her more as each day went by and I got to know more about her.

South Efford held a Christmas party and it was then, that Louisa agreed to go out with me, and we agreed to go together to meet my mum on my birthday.

Louisa and I went to my mum's on my birthday. It's now January 1$^{st}$ 1993, and Louisa recognised my half-brother from school – they were both surprised to see each other. The day went ok.

Two of the girls at work kept coming up to my room without knocking, trying to catch Louisa and I making love, but they never caught us, and I couldn't have a lock on my door, because of fire regulations.

One day Louisa's drunken cousin came to South Efford House, and said he wanted a quiet chat. Basically he came to warn me off Louisa because he wanted to marry her himself, I took no notice of him.

In March I moved out of South Efford House to stay at Louisa's parents' house. I shared a bedroom with Louisa's brother, but I continued to work full-time at South Efford House.

In May, Louisa, who I will call Lou from hereon in, found out she was pregnant. I took her dad on a walk and broke the news to him. He was 6ft 4 and very strong, so I just hoped I'd picked a good day to tell him, but he was fine; we both agreed it would be better if Lou told her mum the news. When Lou told her mum, her mum just said, "Well that makes two of us," so she was ok too, only her mother miscarried at a later date.

At the end of June, Lou and I went down to Salisbury, where my older sister was now living, and while we were on holiday, we decided we wanted to get married. As soon as we got back to Lou's parents, we told them we want to get married; we had to get their approval as Lou was only 17. The parents approved, although Lou's mum said we could not have a church wedding, because Lou's mum was a Jehovah's Witness. We were angry in later months with Lou's mum, because despite denying her daughter a church wedding, saying, "As a Jehovah's Witness, I will not step foot inside a church," just a month after our wedding in a registry office, Lou's mum did in fact go to a friend's church wedding.

Anyway, back to telling Lou's parents we want to get married. Lou's dad was very happy. The next day I went into town and bought Lou a pretty peridot and diamond engagement ring, and our engagement became official.

We had a date set for our wedding – the 14$^{th}$ August '93. Lou's dad, who had a bit of a drink problem back in those days, promised to stay teetotal for that day, until we had gone, and Lou's drunken cousin who wanted to marry Lou, was put in charge of the bar for the day, and told if he got drunk or tried to ruin the day, every guy in the room would beat the crap out of him. So all in all the wedding day went very well; one of the staff from South Efford House, Mary, provided her white Rover as the wedding car, all done up with ribbons. Mary even drove us to a nice spot along Kingsbridge Quay to get some nice photos of us together on the wedding day. Lou's brother William was our best man, and he got into a sticky patch, because I stood up and said my speech before him, and it turned out he had written an identical speech, so he got a bit stuck with what to say for a moment.

Lou and I went on to spend the night at the Motor Lodge in Kingsbridge, overlooking the Quay; we stayed there for bed and breakfast, and got bombarded by seagulls when we went to sit on the patio for breakfast. We did not have a honeymoon, but we were happy with how everything panned out.

Around September, Lou and I were stopped in the village by an old man. He asked if we were, Mr and Mrs Grey. We said yes. He introduced himself as Gilbert Sercombe, he said, "There are some brand new houses being built in Kingston, they will be available in a couple of months, or would you prefer to wait until next year and have a new build in Kingsbridge? They are Housing Association houses, and people in the village have asked me to help you both get a house, with the baby on the way."

We said, "We would like a house in Kingston, please," and in October we were contacted by a housing company offering us the chance to view one of the new houses in Kingston. We couldn't believe our luck. We got our friend Mary to take us over and view the house; it was a nice first home, the area meant we were a bit isolated, but Lou's dad had still got a bit of a drinking problem, and he doesn't know his own strength. He may harm our baby if he picks the baby up when he's drunk, so it's for the best that we move to Kingston, so we accepted the house and were given the keys in November.

We moved in, in November, and one of the residents' daughters from South Efford House gave us lots of furniture and carpets from her mother's bungalow, which was being sold, so we had a bit of a lucky start there too.

Around the same time as we moved, we made more of a serious decision about what our baby would be called. If the baby was to be a girl, then she would be called Charlotte, after a little girl at our wedding.

At our wedding, everyone had moved to the left-hand side of the room, to take photos of us cutting the wedding cake. As we were facing towards the camera, a little voice piped up from beside us, and said, "Don't worry Louisa, you've got Steve now."

She was a sweet little girl called Charlotte, and she is the reason we chose Charlotte for a girl.

The boy's name would prove to be a little more difficult, because I wanted to call our first son Sean, after my best friend at school, only Angela, my boss, had recently lost a grandson called Sean, at only 2 years old. He had bitten through the teat of his dummy in the car, while his dad had gone to pay for petrol, and when the dad came back, Sean had choked to death on the teat, so we thought it would be too much to call our son Sean, as Angela would not have been able to cope. So we popped some names we liked into a hat and drew out the name Aiden.

By Christmas, we had decorated the house the way we wanted and got the cot all ready for when our baby arrives.

We decided to spend Christmas at Lou's parents and while we were at Lou's parents, we decided, as the baby was due on 31st January and we lived out in the sticks without a phone, we would stay at Lou's parents' until the baby was born, in case there are any complications. So we went down the pub New Year's Eve and saw in my birthday.

Now it's January 1st 1994 and I'm now 27 years old.

On January 28th Lou went into labour. Lou's mum came with us; we went to the new maternity ward at Derriford Hospital. If the baby had come two weeks earlier, it would have been born in the old hospital Freedom Fields, where we had been going for all the health checks.

Lou had an epidural and our son was born, just after 7am with a forceps delivery and no other complications on 29th January. We named him Aiden Stephen Grey. Stephen was chosen so Aiden still has my first name, although my real first name is Steve. So many people called me Stephen as I grew up, I just thought we would call him Stephen instead of Steve, so he doesn't get fed up with people calling him by the wrong name, like they do to me. I recall wandering around the hospital while Lou was in labour, with the song, Things Can Only Get Better by D:Ream, going round and round in my head.

I went back to Kingston while Lou was in hospital with Aiden, and I got the heating on, ready for us all to go back to our new home.

It wasn't long after settling in, that we discovered we had the neighbours from hell. The neighbour on our right side would play his music so loud, until 4 or 5am, that the sound would travel through our house to the neighbours on our left, who also had a young baby.

After a couple of weeks of sleepless nights, my left-hand neighbour and I came to the conclusion that our noisy neighbour likes a sleep in on a Sunday morning, so we put speakers outside our houses one Sunday morning, and we both played We Will Rock you by Queen, on full volume. After about ten minutes, my neighbour said, "Quick, turn it off! The police are out the front."

We didn't make a sound, so a policeman went to question a neighbour, who told us after the policeman had gone that even she could hear our neighbour's music at night, so she told the police about our neighbour, rather than the racket we were making. A little old lady popped up from the village to see what all the noise was about, and when she saw both our families had young babies, she said if the neighbour wouldn't stop, she was more than happy to pay for a solicitor, to sort him out.

We went out for a walk one nice sunny day, and discovered a footpath that went in the direction of the sea, so we walked down the path. The place was lovely and so peaceful, you felt you were in a totally different place, even another country. It was just so different. It took you to a quiet little cove – it was lovely.

Our friend Mary, who provided the wedding car, was now godmother of Aiden, and Mary would come and pick us up every other weekend and take us over to Lou's parents for the weekend as we were so isolated where we lived. It was a six-mile round trip on foot to the nearest shops in Modbury just to get one item; it was a bit of a nightmare really. I expect it's ok if you drive a car, though.

Around April, we asked Lou's cousin, who lived on Icy Park, just three doors down from her mum's, if he would like to swap houses with us. After viewing our house, the cousin agreed to swap with us.

In August we swapped houses and moved to Icy Park, and on August $14^{th}$ we had a housewarming /wedding anniversary party.

I had to buy some wooden pallets, to make up some picket fencing to run along the bottom of the garden and to the side of our house, and I had to find some fast-growing bushes, to grow quickly over two glass pits, as the previous tenants threw all their empty bottles in these two pits.

I started working back at South Efford House again.

We spent Christmas Day over with Lou's parents, and had a Christmas drink at the pub.

New Year's Eve, Lou's mum looked after Aiden, while Lou and I went to the pub with Lou's dad to see the New Year in.

It is now 1995 and I am 28 years old.

Lou and I are taking turns going to work at South Efford House.

In February Lou found out she was pregnant again and was due on 5$^{th}$ October.

It was a fairly quiet year up to the birth of our next baby. We still wanted the name Charlotte for a girl, and it was still too soon to call our baby Sean if it was a boy. We watched a quiz show one day, where two men on the panel were called Kieran; we liked that name, and so if we have another boy he will be called Kieran.

Lou went into labour, and we had a trainee doctor to deliver the baby; he only had one hand, so I thought he may find things a little difficult towards the end, but he was a good doctor, with a good bedside manner. The birth went well, although Kieran did end up being born into a bed pan. The trainee doctor did very well, only letting himself down by putting the disposable nappy on Kieran back to front, which gave us all a laugh after a bit of a drawn-out birth.

We now had a chequered double-seated buggy, the front being a pushchair, and the back was a pushchair that converts into a pram, so it was very practical for getting the two boys around in.

Now things have settled down and it's December.

I remembered that the children from our estate, in the summer time, would sit on skateboards and ride down a bit of side road onto the main road through the estate, and there were a number of occasions when drivers had to slam their brakes on before injuring or killing a child. As the side road was directly in line with our house, we were the only people seeing this happen. I said to my wife, "In the summer, when Kieran is born and things have settled down, I will contact the council, and see if they can provide the kids on the estate somewhere safe to play, before one of the kids are killed." So in December I wrote to the council about my concerns, and waited for their reply.

We spent Christmas Day over Lou's parents', and New Year's Day with the usual night out on New Year's Eve and Grandma looking after the children.

It is now January 1996 and I am now 29 years old.

Lou and I go back to taking it in turns to work at South Efford House, depending on who Angela wants. We have been together for two and a half years and all is well.

The council responded to my letter about the children being in danger, and said they had no funds to do anything about it.

I spoke to my boss Angela about it. I said, "As we hold car boot sales at South Efford House in the summer each year, could we hold three in aid of getting a safe play area on Icy Park, before a child is killed? Could we do that this year if I organise it?"

Angela said yes.

I then wrote to local tourist attractions, parks, etc. I asked them if they would donate complimentary tickets, so I could raffle them off to raise more funds.

I found the perfect piece of unused council land on Icy Park where a children's park could be built.

I also put up a petition on the communal notice board on Icy Park, asking those in favour of having a safe play area to be built on Icy Park to sign the petition.

I also contacted Dartington Morris Men, local weavers and spinners, and my old thatching boss and asked if they would come to one of my car boot sales as an added attraction, to draw people in.

Then I wrote back to the council, and said, 'I have organised three car boot sales, I have enclosed a petition, I have written to local attractions to help raise money, and I have found the perfect location on Icy Park to build a children's park. Therefore, would the council consider matching me pound for pound for all the money I raise, to get a park built before a child is killed outside my house?'

About two weeks after sending the letter to the council, I received a phone call from the council saying that £15,000 was available towards a play area on Icy Park, if I can form a residents' association with the council tenants of Icy Park. The council asked me to find a place the council and tenants can meet up, to form a residents' association and discuss the funds and play area in more detail.

I spoke to Angela, and said, "Since we are having car boot sales at South Efford House, could I hold a meeting there for the council and tenants to meet up, so we can form a residents association and secure the £15,000 on offer?"

So Angela agreed to let us hold the meeting there.

I phoned the council back and confirmed a meeting place, and we agreed on a time and date to meet.

Then I contacted the parish council clerk and asked her if the parish council would help with public notices, to inform the residents of Icy Park of the meeting at South Efford House. The clerk said she would get back to me. I gave it two days then rang her back, and she told me the parish council could not help me.

So I put a notice up on Icy Park notice board myself, and I put slips of paper through council tenants' doors on Icy Park, to invite them to the meeting.

The meeting was a success – a residents' association was formed, and I was nominated and seconded to be chairman of the newly formed Icy Park Residents' Association. It was agreed by all present that a safe play area was needed on Icy Park, and we were assured £15,000 was available for this project. Finally we decided to find a venue in the village nearer to Icy Park for all future meetings.

I did get one disappointed hand-delivered letter from a neighbour the next day. The lady was angry that the parish council had put Icy Park play area on their agenda to be discussed at the parish council meeting, the same night as the meeting I had arranged, so she was cross she had attended the wrong meeting. So I just hand wrote a letter back to her, saying the parish council were informed of the meeting, and they said they couldn't help me advertise my meeting, but they knew all about the meeting.

After the meeting, I wrote to the local Gazette to tell them about the newly formed residents association and that we were trying to raise funds for a safe play area. I did it so the council would not go back on their word about the funding and to raise more funds if possible, and raise awareness of the car boot sales at South Efford House. My article was published in the Kingsbridge Gazette on 15/03/96.

I continued my involvement with the tenants and South Hams District Council, and became a member of the tenant's panel, formed by the council, as tenant representative for Aveton Gifford.

I continued to call meetings between the council the tenants and residents of Icy Park. I even held a meeting for parents and children in my back garden, so everyone could go and view the proposed site next to the bottom of my garden, and so the parents and children could see the park's design manager and his folders of play equipment, and they could collectively agree on the play equipment they'd like to see on Icy Park. Everyone agreed on what they would like to have, and the park's design manager took the details back to the council, and in our next residents' association meeting, it was confirmed; the play equipment for Icy Park had been ordered.

About a week later, two longstanding residents of Icy Park put notes through everyone's door on Icy Park, saying they wished to form a new residents' association. I thought, *How petty and stupid, these two people already attended my meetings, now they want to set up a residents' association against an existing one that was doing very well.* But I also thought, *You know what? I am fed up listening to complaints about street lighting, rubbish bins, one way systems and all the other gripes tenants have. I was only ever interested in making sure a child doesn't get killed, I don't need all this other nonsense. Now the play equipment has been ordered and the park site has been approved, no one can change that now, so why don't I just resign as chairman, quit the residents association, and let these two people deal with all the moans and groans? Let them go for my seat; in doing so they will keep the residents' association going long enough to make sure the play park is built, so even if I quit now, I have already won, they're just going to do all the donkey work that goes with it, and I won't miss that for a second.*

So I advertised on the local communal board that I intended to resign at the next meeting, and sure enough these two jumped into my shoes, and did all the hard work for me, without even realising it. They do say those that laugh last, laugh longest.

I continued to be a tenant panel member, partly because I enjoyed it and partly because I knew it would frustrate the hell out of those two residents who just took over the residents' association, that they couldn't actually attend these meetings because they weren't actually council tenants. They were home owners, therefore they couldn't attend these meetings, and you know in the back of their minds they were going to be wondering what goes on in those meetings and what I am up to. I was just having a good time, I don't think they were.

In August, we had three reasons to celebrate. We had our third wedding anniversary, Lou found out she was pregnant again, and the children's park had been completed.

We spent Christmas with Lou's parents again, and celebrated my birthday with them too.

We are now in January 1997 and I am 30 years old.

Lou and I were still working at South Efford House, but Lou stopped in February to take maternity leave.

I was still going to the South Hams District Council's tenants' panel meetings.

I also became very interested in the Referendum Party, and paid to be a member. I even dropped leaflets through people's doors for the Party. The Referendum Party were opposed to joining the European Union, believed our country should have the right to vote on whether we want to join the European Union or not, and the Referendum Party published the many disadvantages of joining the European Union.

Our next baby was due on $5^{th}$ May, but Lou went into labour on the $22^{nd}$ April. At about 5am the contractions started, and this time Lou wanted a home birth. At around 9.30am, I received a telephone call from the Referendum Party, asking if I could gather up some people to hold placards in a photo shoot for the Kingsbridge Gazette, with a member of the Referendum Party, at the Fisherman's Rest in Aveton Gifford. So I said to Lou, "Is it ok to go? Are you ok to be on your own for a while?"

She said, "Yes it's ok."

I rallied round and found some people and we all went down to the Fisherman's Rest, where we were greeted by a man and lady with a very old car, that had 'Referendum Party' written on it, and the car was gleaming. We all stood round the car with placards, with 'Bob Sadler' on some, 'Brussels or Westminster' on others, and 'put Country before Party' on others. The Gazette took the photo, then I shot back home as quickly as possible, getting home around 11am.

We called the midwife, and the midwife came to our home. She brought some gas with her for pain relief, but the bottle didn't work. At around 12pm the midwife phoned another midwife for assistance with the birth. Lou thought as she was carrying different with this pregnancy, and that she would have a girl this time, so we stuck with the name Charlotte and didn't even think of a boy's name.

While the midwife was on the phone calling the other midwife, Lou said she wanted to push and the midwife said, "Ok, just a little push," and with that little push, out shot a little baby boy. Well, the midwife and I were gobsmacked. Lou didn't seem to be in much pain through the labour, and one push and the baby was out – it was all very sudden.

When the midwife went into the kitchen, I said to Lou, "What shall we call him?"

Together we both said, "Sean," and a couple of days later we decided to ask Angela to be Sean and Kieran's godmother, to help her accept Sean, and because she was already like a mother to me, and I know she would try to do her best by our kids, should anything happen to Lou and I.

Lou started to learn to drive and I bought her a black MG Metro; her uncle used to take her on driving lessons. In the summer holidays Lou drove us to Butlin's in Minehead, it was our first family holiday. Her uncle drove the car back to Devon, then brought it back the next Saturday so Lou could drive home again.

On August the 14$^{th}$ we celebrated our fourth wedding anniversary.

The tenants' panel meetings were coming thick and fast as we were going through a consultation period. The council wanted to know if the tenants would prefer to have their houses owned by a private housing company, and they wanted the tenants' panel to look through and discuss the proposals in depth. The tenants' panel agreed the transfer of housing stock to a private company would be much more beneficial to the tenants, so the tenants' panel expressed their view through the tenants' newsletters. In approximately November, the tenants voted whether to stay with the council or transfer to a housing company. The tenants voted to transfer to a housing company.

Christmas was here again; we spent Christmas Day over Lou's parents'. Lou's mum looked after the kids New Year's Eve so we could see in the New Year in the pub.

It is now January 1998 and I'm 31 years old.

Lou and I are still taking turns at working at South Efford House.

In February I won the elections for the central seat, to be a tenant board member for the new housing company which was taking over the council housing stock. The South Hams was split up into five areas, and five tenants from the five areas were elected onto the board. There were also five councillors who joined the board, and between the ten of us, we selected five businessmen to join the board from a long list of applicants. The board chose the name 'South Hams Housing' for the company, but tenants were getting confused between South Hams Housing and South Hams Council Housing, so the company changed names to 'Tor Homes'. I got along well with the tenant board member from Kingsbridge, and as I didn't drive, Pauline, the tenant board member, would give me a lift to the meetings to save my wife from doing double journeys.

In April, Lou and I were walking through Kingsbridge, when we bumped into my mother. She stopped to tell us she had some papers from Social Services at her home, that she thought I may like to see, so we went out to my mum's later to look at these papers. I asked if I could take them away and she said yes.

I wanted to take the papers home, because these were papers held on Social Services records in Amesbury, Wiltshire, about my life in and out of care, and the truth of my life at home and in care was distorted by the records the social worker had made.

The papers were saying that at the age of 9 I was playing truant from school a lot and that I kept running from home. But it gave no reasons for this behaviour.

The fact of the matter was, I was not playing truant at the age of 9, I was being shut under the stairs, or being palmed off onto friends and being withheld from school, due to my back bleeding from being constantly lashed with a belt buckle. I felt deeply offended because the papers also suggested that I was stealing and getting caught by my dad and stepmum, and I didn't like getting told off, so I would play truant or run away. I could not believe it, my dad had fed Social Services a pack of lies to get himself out of trouble, and make me look like the unstable one, the same sick man that got 2 years for sexually abusing my sister for 13 years. I was furious that my life had been recorded in this way, and that, that is the reason my dad got away with all the scars on my back, because the social worker listened to and believed every word my dad said.

To add insult to injury, I had witnessed my dad beat the living daylights out of my stepmum, and I had to put my own life in danger, being really abusive towards my dad and making him chase me, to protect my stepmum and stepsister. I ran to Social Services and demanded I be put in a children's home, and the social worker would not listen to my demand at first, but I insisted. "I will not go back and live with my dad, I will just run away." So by the end of the day, the social worker took me to Orchard House Children's Home in Salisbury.

I was furious to see that the records say my dad put me into care and I was put into Orchard House, it was a twisted truth. When you consider, when it was my turn to see the home manager, my dad was there but the social worker had left. I don't know what my social worker and my dad told the children's home manager, but he sat shouting at me for over a minute, and then said, "Now do you want to go home?" and I said no. I took the home manager by surprise.

When that home manager was leaving Orchard House he took me to one side and said, "You were only supposed to be here for a weekend, then you were supposed to go home, but I stood in and stopped it, I could tell something wasn't right."

So you may be able to tell, that my social worker's reports were making my dad look like an angel, and I was the truant and thief. My dad had to put me in care, I was so bad. My whole childhood had been distorted by my social worker's reports, and that is how my dad got away with lashing the hell out of me and the scars are still clear as day across my back, from his abuse.

I went to Kingsbridge Police and said, "I want to press charges against my dad for the abuse I received as a kid, he's a dangerous, sick man and I have the evidence all over my back, the scars are all still there."

I spent the next 2 years writing to Amesbury Social Services, saying they got their facts wrong. I said I had medicals on entry to each children's home. Why weren't my scars picked up then? And in the children's homes I went swimming with the staff, why did they not see the scars? Orchard House had a pool the whole five years I was there, are you seriously telling me not one member of staff saw my scars? And what about my medical notes in care? Surely someone read them, then they would have known about the scars.

Wasn't it strange, that when I tried the health authorities to try and get my medical records from the ages 0 to 18, they had mysteriously disappeared? No one could find them. A bit convenient, I would say, since I had a care order slapped on me when I was 13 for receiving just £10. No one I have ever heard of got a care order for receiving £10 and clearly marked me as a criminal, worthy of being put into care until I was 18.

Anyway, you can see my frustration, that my dad walked free and I was the one who was punished, and Social Services papers did nothing other than hide the abuse I went through and make me out to be a thief, runaway, and truant without a cause. I mean seriously, how many 9-year-olds do you know that play truant? Where would they hide on a school day? It's just ridiculous, but if you read Social Services papers, that's what I was doing.

Anyway, I carried on arguing my case writing to Salisbury Police and Amesbury Social Services.

While I was taking my frustrations out on the police and Social Services, in other areas of my life, Lou passed her driving test in March, and in the summer holidays we took Lou's parents on holiday with us to Butlin's. It was the first time Lou's parents had gone on holiday in a very long time.

I had resigned from the housing company in late April to deal with Social Services.

I continued to work at South Efford House

Christmas '98 we spent with Lou's parents and we saw New Year's Day in with Lou's parents at their home.

It's now 1999 and I'm 32 years old.

I was still fighting Social Services about their false accounts of my childhood. By the summer, Lou and I decided to move off Icy Park, and in August we swapped houses and moved to Frogmore, but just before we were about to move, our next-door neighbour had a brother, that had had children with my half-sister, and because my half-sister was addicted to drugs, Social Services took her children into care.

When we moved we wrote to Social Services and asked if we could have contact with the children. We felt it was a shame they had gone into care so young.

Not long after we wrote the letter, two social workers turned up at our house, and said, "HI, we are from Social Services. Can we come in for a chat?"

The social workers wanted to know what relation was I to the children's mother, and who my mother was. I told them the name of my half-sister and my mother and they said they had been involved with my mum for quite some time, but she never said she was married before, nor did she say she had any more children. They asked if I had any more brothers and sisters. I said yes, and I told them that I was currently in dispute with Amesbury Social Services over abuse I received as a child, that both my mum and dad were denying to the police. They asked me if I would sign a consent form, for them to look at all records held on the family at Amesbury Social Services, so I said, "Yes, I will."

I signed the consent forms, and they left shortly afterwards.

My wife and I were disgusted to think my mum had hidden all her first family from Devon Social Services, but it was nice to point them in the right direction, after she lied to the police about my abuse, saying she knew nothing about it.

I carried on arguing my case up to Christmas; we

spent Christmas Day at Lou's parents' and New Years' Day at home.

It was now 2000 and I am 33.

I had a letter from Wiltshire Police, saying the Crown Prosecution Service says there is no case, because the photo I sent them of the scars was not very clear, and the belts that I allege my dad hit me with no longer exist, so there is no evidence to support my case.

I was very upset about this, because the police had been handed the belts by my sexually abused sister, but the police never acted on the evidence when it was handed to them. It also meant all the lies in Social Services records in Amesbury stand as true to fact. So I carried on writing to the police and Social Services, until June 2000, when I had a full mental health breakdown, where I was sectioned under the Mental Health Act as a danger to myself. I was just sitting by a lamp post, all confused, waiting for Ellen, one of my ex-girlfriends to arrive, not really of clear mind to know that she didn't even know where I lived. My brain was completely shot to pieces, two policeman had to take me to the police station, and from there, a mental health social worker came and sectioned me, then I was taken to hospital.

I refused medication at the hospital, and all I was doing in my mind was looking for people who were trying to hide my scars so that I could get Social Services to put their paperwork right. By now I was just about suspicious of everyone; I wasn't aware of how ill I was and in the end, staff had to pin me down and inject me. I fell asleep in no time, and when I came round I was very drowsy, but I started to accept the tablets they were giving me.

Two weeks later, the hospital let me back home, and I remained under the psychiatrist with regular visits to the hospital, and had a mental health social worker come and visit me regularly.

As soon as I came out of hospital I binned my two years of correspondence with all authorities to do with my childhood, and focused on getting better for my wife and kids. It took me two years to completely come off risperidone and feel well again. So in the year 2002, I was free of medication, and off the psychiatrists' book, and off the mental health social workers' books too.

Christmas came. We stayed at Lou's parents', and on my birthday we stayed at home.

It's now 2003 and I'm 35 years old.

Lou is pregnant and the baby is due on 3$^{rd}$ March, and it will be a home birth again. This time we changed the name of the baby. If it's a girl, she would now be called Kayleigh, because by accident all three boys had now been given Irish names, so we thought Kayleigh would be more apt now.

On February 20$^{th}$ Lou went into labour; she still hadn't had the baby by time the boys came home from school, so I had to ask a neighbour, whose twins were having a birthday tea as it was their birthday this day, if she could look after our three boys. Later that evening Lou gave birth to a little girl, who we called Kayleigh Louise Grey, taking her mum's first name as her middle name, only it would be Louise instead of Louisa.

In February, I was unemployed, and Lou was on

maternity leave.

In June, Lou went back to work at South Efford House.

In the summer holidays we went camping in Ashburton. Our pitch was just the other side of the stream from where I used to live in a caravan. It was a lovely place for camping, just on the edge of the moors, perfect for going rambling and letting the kids run around and stretch their legs in the fresh air, and the stream behind our tent was perfect for cooling us down on hot days and acting as a fridge for our milk, which we would tie to the trees and place in the water.

In August, Lou started working at Fairfield House Nursing Home in Chillington, as it was closer to our home.

In October we took Lou's parents on holiday to West Bay Holiday Park in Dorset.

In December, Lou's dad became very ill and he had to go to a hospital in London for a heart bypass; he was home for Christmas.

On December 19$^{th}$ Lou and I went to court and declared ourselves bankrupt. We had debts we just couldn't keep up with.

We spent Christmas with Lou's parents, and my birthday.

It is now 2004 and I am 37 years old.

We decided to do a three-way swap, with Lou's parents and her brother, so we could go back to Icy Park, to be close to Lou's dad now he was so ill. Lou's brother had a bungalow on Icy Park that would be ideal for Lou's parents. The housing company turned it into a four-way swap, but we all got to where we wanted to be.

At the beginning of May, we took Lou's mum camping with us to Waterleat Caravan Park.

On the 17$^{th}$ May we all swapped houses and we were now in the house Lou grew up in.

In August, for our 11$^{th}$ wedding anniversary, we took Lou's parents on holiday with us to Tencreek Holiday Park in Looe.

In October, I went back to South Efford House to work for Angela, and to help her move to Paignton, as she was in the process of selling South Efford House.

Angela had moved out by November and the new owners had taken over South Efford House. I didn't get on very well with the new owners, and started to get to such a high stress level that I needed to go back to hospital, and ask to be put back on risperidone. It wasn't that the employers were stressing me out, so much as I discovered I have such a low tolerance for stress that I was going into relapse and desperately needed to get back on 2mg risperidone. I stopped working at South Efford as soon as I went back on the risperidone. I had to see the psychiatrist occasionally, but I didn't need a mental health social worker this time, as I went for help myself.

This Christmas Lou's parents came over to us, as they now had the bungalow, and it was too small to fit everyone in; they also came over for my birthday.

It's now January 2005. I'm now 38 years old and the risperidone is making me feel better.

Lou's dad is not doing very well; he can hardly walk very far, he is very concerned about his heart as well. It was really hard to see him like this, because when he was fit and well, he was forever looking for little jobs to do for people in the village. He was just wasting away. He was scared too, and normally he was a fearless kind of guy, but a gentle giant, who would pick flowers from his garden and take them to the old ladies he worked for in the village.

In May we took Lou's parents to Tencreek Holiday Park, in Looe, and the best Lou's dad could manage was to sit looking out the window towards the sea and watch the boats all day. It was a sad holiday, really, but Lou's dad just kept saying he was happy watching the boats all day. I'm just glad we had a caravan with such a lovely view for Lou's dad.

On June 4$^{th}$ Lou's dad died in hospital. I went to visit him a couple of times on his last days, but I got to the point where I didn't want to see him any worse than he was. I couldn't go back to hospital anymore. I sort of said my goodbyes the last time I saw him, I just felt this was the end, and I didn't really want to see him go, so I couldn't see him anymore.

For the funeral, we arranged it so that the hearse would park outside our house and people could meet up at our house and walk down behind the hearse, to the church. We chose our house, as Lou's dad's home where he was happy and bought up his own family, and everyone knew it as John's house. I met his brothers from Cornwall this day – it was a very memorable day.

Shortly after the funeral Lou's mum said John did not have much money, but with what he had left, she would like to pay for a day out at Woodlands Leisure Park, for all her children and grandchildren. She felt that's what John would have liked to do with the money, gather all the family together and have a special day out, so that's what we all did.

In August we celebrated our 12$^{th}$ wedding anniversary out on the patio John helped me build before he got too ill, and we invited lots of neighbours round for a barbecue.

At Christmas we invited Lou's mum over to ours; we all missed John this Christmas.

We saw in my birthday at home.

It's now January 2006 and I'm 39 years old.

In February we took Lou's mum on holiday to Tencreek Holiday Park, but it wasn't the same without John.

In June I told Lou I was getting fed up at home, could she see if there are any cleaning jobs going at her work? In July a cleaning job became available and I was offered the job, and Lou stayed at home to look after the children.

On August 14$^{th}$ we celebrated our 13$^{th}$ wedding anniversary with a barbecue.

On 2$^{nd}$ December, we took a special trip as a family up to Dingles Fairground Heritage Museum, where they were holding a special event called Night Glow.

The evening was special, because I hadn't seen the Rodeo Switchback built up for 20 years, and it was built up in the museum, to show off to the public. It was a proud moment to show my kids the ride I helped restore and tour with for three years. The ride was not yet ready for public use, but they put all the lights on, on the ride, and it brought back good memories.

We invited Lou's mum over for Christmas and I spent my birthday at home with my family.

It was now January 2007 and I'm now 40 years old.

I am back down to 1mg of risperidone per day, increasing it to 2mg whenever I need to.

In February, I didn't want to work at Fairfield Nursing Home anymore; I had got fed up going round the same routine every day with cleaning, so I asked Lou to go back to caring at the home, so she did.

In the Easter we went on holiday to Looe, to Tencreek Holiday Park with Lou's mum and her uncle, who was now living with her mum.

In August we celebrated our 14th wedding anniversary.

I started to get fed up living in the village, because the nearest town was four miles away, and if I wanted to do voluntary work, I would have to rely on buses that would not get me into town before 10am, once I had dropped our daughter off to school. The children couldn't go to after-school clubs, as the clubs were all four miles away in town, and we could not afford the petrol to take them to clubs. I just felt we were too restricted living in the village. Also thinking about the future, the children would struggle to get work from the village, and college was 20-odd miles away.

Lou was not ready to move on, as she had grown up in the house and all of her memories of her dad were there too. But I did continue to have this conversation with Lou many times.

In the summer holidays we went camping at Woodlands Leisure Park; we got rained off four days through the holiday. The weather got so bad we had to go home, but it was good while it lasted.

In August we celebrated our 15$^{th}$ wedding anniversary.

Lou agreed to go on Home Swapper, so we could try to swap with someone in the town of Kingsbridge.

In October, I was invited by Dingles Fairground Heritage Trust Museum, to come and see the official opening of the Rodeo Switchback. I got permission from the schools to take my children to the museum and have a ride on the Switchback, and all the other old rides in the museum. My old Switchback bosses were there as well, which was nice. My old boss, Stephen, did a speech before the opening, and he even gave me a mention in his speech.

At Christmas Lou's mum and her uncle came over to our house.

It's now January 1$^{st}$ 2009 and I am 42 years old.

As no home swap was coming up for Kingsbridge, I suggested to Lou we look further afield, like near Lifton, where the fairground museum is, so I can go and work there voluntarily. In February someone near Lifton offered us a swap, and then pulled out of it.

We looked at a couple of Kingsbridge houses, but nothing suitable came up.

I said to Lou, "Why don't we try Salisbury? We could live somewhere where the kids can walk to school rather than catch buses, and all amenities will be closer to home, and the town is big enough to suit our needs without being too large." Lou thought it was a good idea too, so I advertised on Home Swapper, that we were looking for Salisbury, and before long, we had a four-way swap set up. The house we viewed was fifteen minutes' walk to the secondary school, and primary school, five minutes' walk from the doctors, and two minutes' walk from the shop. This was absolutely what we were looking for, and with the help of my younger brother and Lou's uncle driving vans for us, we moved to Salisbury on the 1$^{st}$ August.

We deliberately timed the move for the beginning of August to give the children a chance to settle in and get to know the area, before they started school. The boys started making friends on the estate, and settled into school well. Kayleigh struggled to settle in and we had many tearful mornings on the way to school, but this school was much bigger; the old school had 70 pupils, this one had 200 pupils, so it was a bit overwhelming for Kayleigh – she took almost a year to settle in.

Lou started working for a care home in Salisbury two weeks after moving in, as we had set up the job before we moved to Salisbury.

By October, Lou became ill, with a pain in her right side in the pelvis. Lou initially thought it was a water infection, but it turned out not to be the case, and by November Lou had to take sick leave from work.

Kieran had to be tested for coeliac disease, because the doctor was concerned about his weight and height.

Further investigations confirmed Kieran does actually have coeliac disease, with means he is allergic to wheat and gluten, and so he has to have food like bread and crackers on prescription. We all got tested for coeliac disease, but Kieran is the only one that has it.

Christmas came. Lou's mum and uncle didn't come up until a couple of days after Christmas, because Lou's mum is a Jehovah's Witness again and doesn't celebrate Christmas, but we do leave the Christmas tree and decorations up, and we continue to celebrate Christmas through to the New Year.

It's January 1$^{st}$ 2010 and I am 43 years old.

After Christmas I worked voluntarily for a while at the Trussel Trust Food Bank, which makes food parcels for poor families, who are in need of emergency food supplies.

In the Easter Holidays we went down to Devon and stayed in a friend's house, and the boys stayed at their friends' houses for the week. Fortunately for Kieran, his best friend that he stayed with also has coeliac disease, so he knew his food would be safe there.

After the Easter Holidays, I saw the doctor about completely coming off risperidone, and she agreed to let me come off them.

In April I started work at Glenside Hospital, just outside Salisbury, as a domestic. Within three weeks, I had to stop working there, as Lou was in so much pain, and on such a high dose of medication to fight the pain, she could hardly walk anywhere, and she couldn't look after the children at all, so Lou had to apply for Employment Support Allowance.

By July I was really ill mental health-wise, and I was not aware of it myself. The mental health crisis team had to be called in and I had to see the doctor and take diazepam, to help me sleep and go back on to 2mg of risperidone a day.

In July, Lou was turned down for Employment Support Allowance, so she had to appeal against their decision.

In August we celebrated our 17$^{th}$ wedding anniversary.

In September, Aiden was happy as he started his mechanics course, at Salisbury College, which is what he really wanted to do at the time.

At Christmas Lou lost her appeal for Employment Support Allowance, and her money was stopped. I had to apply for Jobseekers Allowance, regardless of the fact that Lou was too ill to look after the children.

Our Christmas was somewhat dampened by the Employment Support Allowance decision.

The Trussel Trust Food Bank lifted our spirits though as they bought around a Christmas hamper. I wrote a letter to say thank you, and asked them if they would go to the Children's Home, Orchard House, and give those children a hamper. It would mean a lot to them, so they did.

One thing was nice at Christmas – through Facebook, I'd managed to get in contact with all my proper brothers and sisters, and through Facebook we were all able to say happy Christmas to each other on Christmas Day, and that has not happened since I was 9 years old. I even got to say happy Christmas to my foster sisters as well.

Lou's mum and uncle came to stay after Christmas for a week.

January the 1st is here again, it's 2011 and I am 44 years old.

The boys had all stayed up for the first time to see in the New Year and my birthday; we pulled Christmas crackers at midnight, and woke up Kayleigh, who felt left out because we didn't get her down to pull a cracker, so we pulled one with her as well.

The children all went back to school and I started to look for work.

In March I finally got offered a temporary job at my children's school, assisting the school caretaker. I took a couple of days off three weeks into the job due to picking up a virus from my daughter. A week after returning to the school I had to call in sick again, due to a problem with my back for the first time ever, and if the caretaker had had proper health and safety training, I would not have been off with a bad back. The bad back was caused by pulling round fully loaded table carrying trolleys – they were so heavy when fully loaded, that I actually bruised the back of my legs, having to put a foot on the wall, and pulling the trolley with all my might, to get the trolley up a slope. My back just went when I got up one morning, after a few days of pulling these trolleys round. I had bruises at the back of my legs for a week, from pulling these trolleys on my own and putting them into storage. The trolleys were designed with handles at both ends to be pushed and pulled by two people, but the caretaker never helped me, so when my wife went into the school later and informed them of my back trouble, they said they no longer needed me and I was laid off. So my job was over in April and I had to go back to the Job Centre and apply for Jobseekers Allowance.

From April to August, I went to many interviews or had telephone interviews, mainly for cleaning jobs, but I was never successful, and even the Job Centre makes you feel like a criminal for not having a job, regardless of how hard you try. By August I was so stressed I had to go to my doctor and have my risperidone increased to 2 ½ mg, as I was feeling very ill. I also started claiming Employment Support Allowance, instead of Jobseekers Allowance.

2 ½mg risperidone was not enough, I had to have the dosage increased to 3mg per day. I also had to take diazepam to help me sleep. It took about three weeks to get my mind stabilised. I could not face another day at the Job Centre being treated like a criminal for not having a job, and I was trying my best, looking at job sites on the internet a minimum of twice a day, and getting nowhere. It just made me so ill, the whole system, filling in forms to prove you have looked for work, and writing down rejection after rejection when it comes, for jobs applied for.

After two and a half months on 3mg risperidone per day, I started to feel better, but my wife started taking a turn for the worse. She was in so much pain she was having to stay in bed all day, for three or four days at a time, so I told my wife we would have to stop my claim for Employment Support Allowance, and start a fresh claim for her.

As Lou is so ill, I can't apply for work, while Lou genuinely can't look after our four children. She hasn't cooked for them for well over a year because she is in too much pain to stand that long; she does no household chores, she just sits curled up in a ball on the sofa, or lies in bed in pain all day.

I thought I would write my life story. I would love to see it made into a film, to show politicians and the Government, some of us genuinely do come from a bad upbringing, and poor childhood, and it can have a knock-on effect later in life, like me needing risperidone, and that my wife is genuinely ill as well. I know that we will have to fight to keep Employment Support Allowance again; they will say my wife is fit for work again, when she is genuinely ill. We have had it hard enough, so I wanted to write my story, because there are thousands of kids that have been through the care system, that struggle to get work and make family life work. The Job Centre and the Government need to stop treating us like criminals, and the Government need to realise, kids that grew up in care are at a genuine disadvantage, right from the start, and their life in care could follow them for the rest of their life, like mine has, making me need risperidone 3mg a day, just to appear normal to everyone else.

There should be more support for children that come out of care, there should be more support for people who have developed mental health issues, and there should be more understanding in Job Centres. We are not all equal; many kids from care are truly disadvantaged. They don't have family support, they don't have a good education, and it's not our fault.

I believe I have written a fairly unique story in some ways, but in other ways, I believe there are thousands of young adults who come out of care, who can relate to my story in care. I don't believe there is a book or film like this anywhere, but we need one, to open the Government's eyes to a little taste of reality.

This is my true life story,
by Steve Kieran Sean Grey.

Printed in Great Britain
by Amazon